Praise for *Badge of Horror*

Sarah K., Paranormal Book Club ★★★★☆ DiBacco delivers a captivating supernatural thriller that had me up well past midnight. The chemistry between vampire detective Angelo and witch Andrea sizzles from their first meeting, developing organically amid the chaos of ritual murders and ancient vampire politics. New Orleans comes alive as more than just a setting—it's practically a character itself, with DiBacco expertly weaving local folklore into the supernatural fabric of the story. While the middle section drags slightly with exposition about vampire hierarchies, the final confrontation with Sapphira is worth the wait. What truly elevates this novel is Angelo's internal struggle between his vampire nature and his desire to protect innocents. I'm already eager for the sequel hinted at in the epilogue!

Michael T., Fantasy Review ★★★★★ As someone who thought vampire detectives had been done to death, I'm thrilled to say "Badge of Horror" breathes new life into the subgenre. DiBacco creates a richly layered supernatural society operating beneath New Orleans' tourist-friendly veneer, complete with complex politics and long-standing feuds. The police procedural elements feel authentic, and Angelo's methods of hiding his vampiric nature while utilizing it to solve crimes are cleverly conceived. The standout element is the relationship between Angelo and Andrea—their supernatural backgrounds should make them enemies, yet their shared sense of justice creates a foundation for something deeper. The novel balances action, romance, and worldbuilding masterfully, culminating in a finale that satisfies while cleverly setting up future installments. This is urban fantasy at its finest.

Jennifer L., College Student ★★★☆☆ "Badge of Horror" shows promise but falls into some familiar paranormal detective tropes. DiBacco's New Orleans setting feels authentic and atmospheric, and the central mystery—involving ritualistic killings tied to an ancient vampire—creates genuine tension. However, the romance between Angelo and Andrea develops too quickly to be entirely believable, even with their supernatural connection. The novel's strongest elements are its crime scenes and Angelo's detective work, which showcase DiBacco's talent for procedural details. Some secondary characters, particularly Captain Rhemann, deserve more development, though the epilogue suggests this will come in future books. While not breaking new ground in the paranormal detective genre, it's an entertaining read for fans of supernatural mysteries set in evocative locations.

Robert J., Horror Fan Allauthor.com ★★★★☆ DiBacco knows how to write genuinely unsettling horror within an urban fantasy framework. The murder scenes are described with chilling detail without becoming gratuitously graphic, and antagonist Sapphira ranks among the most terrifying vampires I've encountered in recent fiction—her calculating cruelty and ancient power make her a formidable villain. The novel occasionally gets sidetracked with romantic elements that lighten the tension, but it always returns to the central horror narrative with renewed intensity. The climactic supernatural confrontation in the catacombs beneath New Orleans is a masterclass in suspenseful writing. What prevents this from being a five-star review is an occasionally uneven pace, but DiBacco has established himself as a voice to watch in supernatural horror. This badge definitely earns its horror credentials.

BADGE OF HORROR

Kevin B. DiBacco

© Copyright 2025 by Kevin B. DiBacco

This book is a work of fiction. Names, characters, businesses, places, events, conversations, opinions, and incidents are either products of the author's imagination or are used fictitiously. Any resemblance to actual events, locales, conversations, opinions, business establishments, or persons, living or dead, is entirely coincidental and unintended.

All rights reserved. No part of this book may be reproduced in whole or in part without written permission from the publisher except by reviewers who may quote brief excerpts in connection with a review in a newspaper, magazine or electronic publication; nor may any part of this book be reproduced, stored in a retrieval system or transmitted in any form or by any means electronic, mechanical, photocopying, recording or any other means, without written permission from the publisher.

About the Author

37 years behind the camera/editing/producing & directing.Over 600 Television Commercials, 4 Documentaries, a dozen Music Videos, MTV aired Music Videos, dozens of Broadcast and Cable TV programs, and 5 feature films.Winner of the Houston International Film Festival
1990 Broderson AD Club of Maine Award
1999 4 Connecticut Association of Broadcasting Awards
5 Maine Association of Broadcasting Awards

https://filmakerim.tripod.com/kevindibacco.html

Table of Contents

Prologue 9
Chapter 1 Night Shift 12
Chapter 2: Shadows of the Heart 17
Chapter 3: Shadows of the Past 25
Chapter 4: Innocence Lost 28
Chapter 5: Confrontation in the projects 34
Chapter 6: The Weight of Centuries 37
Chapter 7: A grizzly discovery 40
Chapter 8: Sunrise and secrets 44
Chapter 9: Whispers in the Dark Wave 46
Chapter 10: Clash in the Flower Shop 51
Chapter 11: The Summons 56
Chapter 12: The Decision 59
Chapter 13 The Captains Confession 62
Chapter 14: Echoes of Cruelty 68
Chapter 15: Planning the Rebellion 80
Chapter 16: Charting a Course 85
Chapter 17: Shadows in the Florist Shop 89
Chapter 18: Shadows of the Night 91
Chapter 19: Confronting the Unstoppable 94
Chapter 20: The Gathering Storm 100
Chapter 21: The Trial of Sapphira 108
Chapter 22: The Maelstrom of Magic and Will 113
Chapter 23: The Dawn of a New Era 119
Epilogue: A New Dawn 123

Prologue

The air hung thick with the scent of blood and gunpowder; a pungent reminder of the battle that had raged mere days ago. As night fell over the battered city, most of its inhabitants huddled in their homes, whispering prayers of gratitude for their survival and mourning those lost in the conflict. But in the shadows of the French Quarter, a different sort of war was about to begin.

Sapphira LeCroix stood atop St. Louis Cathedral, her lithe figure silhouetted against the storm-wracked sky. Lightning illuminated her face, revealing features of otherworldly beauty twisted into a triumphant sneer. She breathed deeply, savoring the fear that permeated the air like a fine perfume.

"Can you taste it, my dear?" she purred to the figure kneeling beside her. "The delicious tang of mortal terror?"

The man at her feet – barely more than a boy, really – raised his head, revealing eyes that glowed an unnatural shade of amber. "Yes, mistress," he replied, his voice hoarse with hunger.

Sapphira laughed, the sound cutting through the rumble of thunder. "Then rise, Angelo. Rise and take your place as my chosen one."

As Angelo Dubois stood on shaky legs, the last vestiges of his humanity slipping away, he caught sight of his reflection in a rain-slicked gargoyle. His once-warm brown skin had taken on an ashen hue, and razor-sharp fangs peeked out from behind his lips. He was no longer the idealistic young soldier who had arrived in New Orleans just weeks ago. Now, he was something else entirely.

Sapphira's cold hand cupped his cheek, forcing him to meet her gaze. "You are reborn, my child. Stronger, faster, immortal. Together, we shall rule this city for eternity."

But as Angelo looked out over the city he had once sworn to protect, he felt not elation but a deep, gnawing dread. What had he become? And at what cost?

New Orleans, Present Day

The sultry night air clung to Angelo's skin as he made his way down Bourbon Street, the sounds of jazz and revelry fading into the background. Two centuries had passed since his transformation, and while his physical appearance remained frozen in time, his eyes now held the weight of lifetimes lived.

A sudden gust of wind carried an intoxicating scent his way - jasmine, mixed with something...magical. Intrigued, he traced the scent to a small flower shop tucked away on a side street. The bell above the door chimed softly as he entered, surrounding him with a riot of colors and fragrances.

"We're closed," a melodious voice called from the back of the shop.

"My apologies," Angelo replied, his keen eyes scanning the dimly lit interior. "I'm Detective Dubois. I'm investigating some strange occurrences in the area and was hoping to ask a few questions."

A woman emerged from behind a curtain of hanging plants, her green eyes narrowing as they fell upon Angelo. She was striking, with raven hair and an aura that spoke of old magic.

"Andrea Deveraux," she said, extending her hand. "And 'strange occurrences' is a relative term in New Orleans, Detective."

As their hands touched, a jolt of electricity seemed to pass between them. Andrea's eyes widened in surprise, and Angelo felt his long-dead heart give a phantom leap.

"You're not human," they both said in unison, then laughed, breaking the tension.

"Witch," Andrea admitted with a wry smile.

"Vampire," Angelo countered, raising an eyebrow.

For a moment, they simply regarded each other, centuries of ingrained caution warring with an undeniable attraction. Despite their different ancestries - Andrea from a long line of witches, Angelo turned by Sapphira herself - there was an unmistakable spark between them.

"Well, Detective," Andrea finally said, her voice warm with amusement, "why don't you tell me about these strange occurrences? I might be able to... shed some light on the situation."

As Angelo began to explain the recent string of supernatural disturbances, neither could shake the feeling that their meeting was more than mere coincidence. Little did they know that the forces set in motion centuries ago by Sapphira were stirring once again, and their newfound connection would soon be tested in ways they could never imagine.

The winds of change were blowing through New Orleans once more, carrying with them the scent of jasmine, the promise of danger, and the first whispers of a love that would challenge the very foundations of their world.

Chapter 1 Night Shift

The scent of fresh blood cut through the humid New Orleans night, a siren song that Angelo Dubois had spent centuries learning to resist.

The street was silent aside from a few drunk stragglers making their way home from Bourbon Street. Detectives rarely arrived at fresh murder scenes this early — but Angelo Dubois wasn't like most detectives. He preferred working the night shift. Shadows and darkness were his home as much as the glowing neon lights of the French Quarter.

When Angelo stepped out of his black vintage Camaro, the newbie officers straightened up. His imposing figure demanded attention. Standing at 6'2" with sharp features and piercing grey eyes, Angelo had an air of dangerous confidence.

"What do we got?" Angelo asked gruffly as he approached the alleyway littered with flashing police lights.

"Twenty-Six-year-old female. Name is Karen Wright. Looks to have been strangled from behind, but there's hardly any other injuries or signs of struggle," replied Officer Hayes, a rookie who still seemed shaken by his first homicide case.

Angelo pulled on a pair of sunglasses before stepping around the crime scene photographer and kneeling beside the victim. Her jet-black hair was strewn wildly across her face. Deep purple bruises in the shape of fingers marked her slender neck. Angelo noted two tiny puncture wounds hidden underneath the marks from her killer's grasp. He frowned slightly. This wasn't public knowledge, but Karen was the third young woman murdered in New Orleans this month. And the murderer wasn't human. Angelo focused intensely on the victim's neck wounds. His centuries of experience told him those were vampire bites - yet the actual cause of death was strangulation, not blood loss. Whoever killed Karen didn't fully feed on her or turn her. He leaned in close enough to detect a faint scent still lingering in her hair...animal fur, pine trees and something mineral he couldn't place. An odd mix of smells for a young woman who seemed to be a typical city dweller. Pulling a small UV penlight from his pocket, Angelo discreetly shone it over the rest of Karen's skin. There on the inside of her left wrist was a rash of tiny scars. Defensive wounds from another vampire who had tried to subdue her. He had seen those kinds of evenly spaced scars many times before. Who was so desperately trying to cover their tracks?

Angelo quickly weighed whether to tell his colleagues the truth - that they were likely dealing with another murderous Creole vampire using New Orleans as his own personal hunting ground. But his undead status was not exactly public record. The other cops would never believe the intricacies of what these bite marks, scars and smells showed. He would have to solve Karen's murder quietly using his own contacts amongst the city's hidden supernaturals. This was the complex dance that came with being the only vampire detective: in New Orleans bringing justice while discreetly protecting the secrets of his own kind. As he stared down at Karen's lifeless body, Angelo hoped he could do both before the rising body count attracted too much unwanted attention from the human authorities...or worse, the cruel elder council that truly ruled over the New Orleans vampire clans.

As Angelo left the crime scene, Captain Rhemann approached him. "Interesting case, Dubois," he said, his eyes lingering on the victim's neck. "Anything... unusual to report?" Angelo hesitated, sensing something off about Rhemann's tone. "Nothing concrete yet, sir. I'll keep you posted." Rhemann nodded, a knowing glint in his eye. "See that you do. Some cases in this city ... well, let's just say they're not always what they seem."

Angelo absently twisted the ancient lapis lazuli ring on his finger—a Dubois family heirloom that held secrets far beyond its brilliant blue stone—before pulling his coat tighter and stepping into the night."

Angelo left the crime scene and headed straight for the French Quarter. Marie Levesque's little herb shop was concealed down an alley so narrow a car couldn't fit. He approached the weathered red door, the entrance barred to human eyes by protective charms.

He didn't bother knocking - Marie already knew. "Get in here, vampire," her raspy voice called out. The shop smelled pungent, an odd mix of incense and dried magnolias. Lining the walls were jars filled with unidentifiable plants, bones and powders. The elderly witch peered out from behind stacks of heavy spell books. "To what do I owe the pleasure?" she grinned, showing her one remaining yellow tooth. Despite the cordiality, Angelo knew Marie and the other New Orleans witches still harbored plenty of distrust towards vampires. Centuries of conflict left deep wounds.

"A young woman was killed last night. Same M.O. as the last two - strangulation marks along with twin vampire bites," Angelo explained. "And she had defensive scars that could only come from one of us."

Marie closed her eyes, beginning to chant softly. Angelo recognized a locator incantation meant to identify supernatural energies around last night's murder scene. A few minutes later, she opened her eyes with a frustrated sigh. "There was magic there. Faint but unmistakable...some kind of cloaking spell meant to hide traces from vampires. And it has Creole witchcraft written all over it," she revealed ominously. "Your kind and mine have an unfortunate killer lurking among us."

Angelo clenched his jaw. This complicated things. A vampire and witch working together, expertly covering their tracks? His pursuit just got much more dangerous...but his determination only grew.

"Why kill these women if not for blood?" Marie questioned, perplexed. "Strangulation seems...intimate. Personal. And violent for our kind." Angelo considered the implications. His kind could rip out a human's throat easily enough if bloodlust overtook them. Strangulation took effort - sustained, intimate effort while feeling the victim's last pulses and gasps. This hinted at a dark and twisted psyche behind the kills.

"I caught the scent of pine, fur and minerals on the latest victim. Traces from wherever she was kept before her death," Angelo said. "My bet is our killer is dragging them from the Quarter, out to some remote cabin or cave." Marie shuffled through an ancient map collection, scanning for remote forest areas near Louisiana's pine lands. She circled an isolated ridge northeast of the city.

"There. Miles from any main roads or towns. Remote enough for prison spells so no screams can escape," she suggested ominously. "The minerals…could be rare iron deposits that would hamper mystical detection." Angelo felt they had found the monster's lair. Now to actually confront who - or what - awaited there. "I know you don't want human cops, or the Elder Council involved yet … so what's your plan?" Marie asked. Angelo gave a wry smile, baring his fangs slightly. "Simple. I pay our killer a personal visit … vampire to vampire."

Angelo veered his sleek black Camaro off the last small rural town's main route onto a dirt backroad. His headlights cut through looming oak trees and dense forest as he raced towards the secluded wooded ridge Marie had uncovered. He didn't pass a single car or building for forty miles. The moonless night and cloudy sky made it pitch black, but his vampire vision could see the path clearly.

When Angelo caught sight of the small wooden cabin nestled amongst the pine trees, he killed the engines and lights. A regular human couldn't have spotted the remote shelter - but through the dark, Angelo observed tendrils of smoke wafting from the chimney. His target was inside. Moving with preternatural speed, Angelo approached silently from downwind. He couldn't risk the other vampire hearing or scenting him prematurely. Crouching below a window, he heard the telltale heartbeat of a human woman - terrified, erratic. So, his killer had already taken another victim.

Angelo would need the element of surprise on his side. He stealthily ripped a side door off its hinges and burst into the room, fangs bared, and claws extended for a fight. "Release her!" he commanded with a roar. The site that greeted him was far more horrendous than he expected. This was no ordinary vampire...

Chapter 2: Shadows of the Heart

The soft glow of the antique desk lamp cast long shadows across Angelo's office. Outside, the sultry New Orleans night pulsed with its usual blend of jazz, laughter, and the faint whisper of secrets best left untold. Angelo leaned back in his chair, loosening his tie as he gazed at the framed photo on his desk. It was a candid shot from last year's Mardi Gras, capturing a moment of shared laughter between him and Andrea.

His fingers traced the edge of the frame, a small smile playing on his lips as he remembered their first meeting. It had been a night much like this one, thick with humidity and the promise of adventure...

Three Years Ago

The crime scene was a mess of shattered glass and overturned furniture. At its center lay the body of Thomas Beauregard, local antiques dealer and, if Angelo's sources were correct, dabbler in magical artifacts. The coroner was examining the body, but Angelo's keen nose had already picked up the acrid scent of dark magic.

"Detective Dubois," a uniformed officer called out, "there's someone here insisting on seeing the body. Says she's a consultant."

Angelo turned, his eyebrows rising as he took in the woman striding purposefully towards him. She was striking, with raven hair and eyes that seemed to spark with an inner fire. But it was the subtle aura of power surrounding her that truly caught his attention. Witch, his instincts whispered.

"I'm Andrea Deveraux," she said, extending her hand. "I was called in to consult on this case."

Angelo shook her hand, noting the warmth of her skin against his perpetually cool touch. "I wasn't informed of any consultants, Ms. Deveraux."

Her eyes narrowed slightly. "That's because the captain called me directly. He thought this case might benefit from my ... unique perspective."

Understanding dawned. Captain Rhemann must have sensed the supernatural elements at play. "I see," Angelo said carefully. "And what perspective might that be?"

Andrea leaned in close, her voice dropping to a whisper. "The kind that recognizes when a man has been killed by a cursed object rather than a human assailant."

Angelo's eyes widened fractionally. It seemed Ms. Deveraux was more than just a pretty face. "Well then," he said, gesturing towards the body, "shall we?"

As they worked the scene together, Angelo found himself impressed by Andrea's keen observations and magical knowledge. She moved with confidence, her fingers tracing sigils in the air that revealed hidden magical traces.

"There," she said, pointing to a shattered display case. "That's where the cursed object was kept. See the residual energy pattern?"

Angelo nodded, marveling at the swirling colors only visible to those with supernatural sight. "Can you tell what kind of object it was?"

Andrea's brow furrowed in concentration. "Something small... a piece of jewelry, maybe? The energy signature is old, incredibly old. Pre-colonial, if I had to guess."

Something small... a piece of jewelry, maybe? The energy signature is old, incredibly old. Pre-colonial, if I had to guess. It reminds me of the protective amulets my grandmother used to craft, drawing on our family's ancient magical lineage.

"Any idea who might have taken it?" Angelo asked, already mentally cataloging potential suspects in the supernatural underground.

Andrea shook her head. "Not yet, but I have some contacts who might be able to help. I'll need to do some research, cross-reference with known cursed artifacts from that period."

Angelo found himself smiling. "Well, Ms. Deveraux, it seems we have our work cut out for us."

"Please," she said, returning his smile with one that made his long-still heart give a phantom leap, "call me Andrea."

The Beauregard case had been just the beginning. Over the next few months, Angelo and Andrea found themselves working together more and more frequently. Their complementary skills made them a formidable team, and Angelo couldn't deny the growing attraction he felt towards the brilliant witch.

There was the case of the haunted jazz club on Frenchmen Street, where Andrea's quick thinking and powerful protection spell had saved Angelo from a possessed saxophone intent on decapitation. He could still remember the feel of her hand in his as she pulled him to safety, the way her eyes had shone with a mixture of concern and exhilaration.

Then there was the werewolf pack causing trouble in the Bayou, where Angelo's vampire strength and Andrea's calming magic had prevented an all-out supernatural war. They'd spent hours trudging through the swamp, trading quips and personal stories. It was then that Angelo had first opened up about his long, often lonely existence as a vampire.

"Don't you ever get tired of it?" Andrea had asked, her voice soft with empathy. "Watching the world change around you while you stay the same?"

Angelo had been silent for a long moment before answering. "Sometimes," he admitted. "But then I remember all the good I can do with this gift – or curse, depending on how you look at it. And lately ..." he trailed off, glancing at her before quickly looking away.

"Lately?" Andrea prompted.

"Lately, I've found reasons to be glad of my longevity," he finished, hoping she couldn't see the way his face would have flushed if he'd been human.

As they worked case after case together, Angelo found himself looking forward to each new adventure, not just for the thrill of the hunt, but for the chance to spend more time with Andrea. He admired her quick wit, her compassion, and the way she fearlessly faced down threats that would send most humans running.

But it was the Midnight Massacre case that truly cemented their bond.

The warehouse was eerily silent as Angelo and Andrea crept through its shadowy interior. They'd been tracking a rogue vampire for weeks, one responsible for a string of brutal killings that threatened to expose the supernatural world to human scrutiny.

"I don't like this," Andrea whispered, her fingers curled around a glowing protective charm. "It feels like we're walking into a trap."

Angelo nodded, every one of his heightened senses on high alert. "Stay close," he whispered.

They'd barely taken another step when a blur of motion erupted from the darkness. Angelo reacted instantly, shoving Andrea behind him as he met the attack head-on. The rogue vampire was incredibly strong, driven mad by bloodlust and dark magic.

The fight was a whirlwind of supernatural speed and strength. Angelo could hear Andrea chanting behind him, feel the buildup of magical energy as she prepared a spell. But before she could release it, the rogue broke through Angelo's guard, its claws raking across his chest.

Angelo stumbled back with a pained growl, giving the rogue the opening it needed to lunge at Andrea. Time seemed to slow as Angelo saw those deadly claws reaching for her throat.

"No!" he roared, summoning every ounce of his vampiric speed. He threw himself between Andrea and the attack, feeling those claws sink deep into his back. But the moment's distraction was all Andrea needed.

With a cry of power, she unleashed her spell. Brilliant white light exploded from her hands, engulfing the rogue vampire. It shrieked in agony as the purifying magic tore through its corrupted form, reducing it to ash in seconds.

As the light faded, Angelo sagged against Andrea, his wounds already beginning to heal but leaving him weak from blood loss. She lowered him gently to the ground, cradling his head in her lap.

"You idiot," she choked out, tears glimmering in her eyes. "Why did you do that? I had the spell ready!"

Angelo managed a weak smile. "Couldn't risk it," he murmured. "Couldn't let you get hurt."

Andrea's hand cupped his cheek, her touch sending a jolt through him that had nothing to do with his injuries. "Angelo," she whispered, her face drawing closer to his.

For a moment, the world seemed to hold its breath. Angelo could see every fleck of gold in Andrea's green eyes, could feel the warmth of her breath ghosting across his lips. His gaze dropped to her mouth, and he found himself lifting his head slightly, drawn by an irresistible force.

Their lips were a hairsbreadth apart when the sound of approaching sirens shattered the moment. Andrea pulled back, her cheeks flushed as she helped Angelo to his feet.

"We should go," she said, not quite meeting his eyes. "Can you walk?"

Angelo nodded, trying to ignore the ache in his chest that had nothing to do with his healing wounds. "Yeah, I'm okay. Let's get out of here."

As they slipped away into the night, Angelo couldn't help but wonder what might have happened if those sirens hadn't interrupted them. And judging by the way Andrea's hand lingered on his arm as they walked, he suspected he wasn't the only one.

In the months that followed, Angelo found his thoughts returning to that moment in the warehouse with increasing frequency. He'd catch himself staring at Andrea during their planning sessions, admiring the way her brow furrowed in concentration or how her eyes lit up when she solved a particularly challenging magical puzzle.

But with those thoughts came a growing sense of unease. He was a vampire, immortal and bound to the night. She was a witch, powerful and very much alive. How could he even consider pursuing a relationship with her?

And yet, the pull he felt towards Andrea was undeniable. It wasn't just physical attraction, though he certainly found her beautiful. It was the way she challenged him, pushed him to be better. The way she saw past his vampire nature to the man beneath. The way she made him feel, for the first time in centuries, truly alive.

One night, as they pored over ancient texts in Andrea's cozy apartment, Angelo found himself watching her instead of the dusty pages before him. She was wearing a simple oversized sweater, her hair pulled back in a messy bun, and he thought she'd never looked more beautiful.

"You're staring," Andrea said without looking up from her book.

Angelo blinked, embarrassed at being caught. "Sorry, I was just... thinking."

Now Andrea did look up, her eyebrow raised quizzically. "About what?"

He hesitated, weighing his words carefully. "About us," he finally admitted. "About... what we are to each other."

Andrea's expression softened, a mix of hope and uncertainty in her eyes. "And what are we, Angelo?"

He stood, moving to sit beside her on the small couch. "Partners," he began. "Friends. But..." he trailed off, struggling to find the right words.

Andrea turned to face him fully, her knee brushing against his thigh. "But?" she prompted gently.

Angelo took a deep, unnecessary breath. "But I can't help feeling like we could be more. Like we should be more." He reached out, taking her hand in his. "Andrea, I... I care for you. More than I've cared for anyone in a very long time."

Andrea's fingers intertwined with his, her thumb tracing small circles on his skin. "I care for you too, Angelo," she whispered. "But..."

"But I'm a vampire and you're a witch," he finished for her, a sad smile on his face.

She nodded. "It's not just that. Our worlds are so different. The dangers we face... I don't know if I could bear losing you."

Angelo brought his free hand up to cup her cheek, his touch feather-light. "I'm not going anywhere," he promised. "Whatever comes, we'll face it together."

For a long moment, they sat there in silence, the air between them charged with unspoken emotion. Then, slowly, inevitably, they began to lean towards each other.

Just as their lips were about to meet, Andrea's phone rang, startling them both. She pulled back with a nervous laugh, reaching for the device.

"Deveraux," she answered, her voice slightly breathless. As she listened to the caller, her expression grew serious. "We'll be right there."

She hung up, turning to Angelo with a mixture of regret and determination. "That was Captain Rhemann. There's been another murder, looks like our kind of case."

Angelo nodded, pushing down his disappointment. "Duty calls," he said, standing and offering her his hand. "Shall we?"

As they gathered their things and headed out into the night, Angelo couldn't help but feel that something had shifted between them. The air was thick with possibility and unspoken promises. Whatever the future held, he knew that his fate was now inextricably linked with Andrea's.

Back in the present, Angelo set down the photo with a soft sigh. So much had changed since that first meeting, and yet so much remained unresolved. He and Andrea had danced around their feelings for months now, neither quite brave enough to take that final step.

But as he stood, preparing to head out for another night of supernatural crime-solving, Angelo made a silent vow. No more hesitation, no more holding back. Life – or in his case, unlife – was too short to waste on fear and doubt. Whatever obstacles lay ahead, he would face them with Andrea by his side. As partners, as friends, and hopefully, as something more.

With a determined set to his shoulders, Angelo grabbed his coat and headed out into the New Orleans night. There were monsters to catch and a city to protect. And just maybe, a love story to finally begin.

Chapter 3: Shadows of the Past

As Angelo merged into the bustling nightlife of the city, his phone buzzed again. This time, it was a call from dispatch with an address - secluded, on the outskirts of town. With a sense of foreboding, he turned his car onto a narrow dirt road, the headlights cutting through the encroaching darkness. As he approached the location, the night's silence was suddenly shattered by blood-curdling screams echoed through the forest as Angelo burst into the cabin, unprepared for the nightmare that awaited him. The sight inside the cabin was beyond gruesome. Three women chained, tortured, and drained of life-force. Towering above them was Jacques LeRouge, blood dripping from his fangs as he turned to Angelo with a wicked grin. "My old friend! Come to end our games so soon? The fun's just beginning..." A female vampire emerged from the shadows then, stunning and ancient symbols carved into her very flesh. Her presence filled the room with a palpable sense of power and dread. "May I present my new progeny, Sapphira," Jacques purred, gesturing to his protege. "She shows such delicious... promise." "You always did prefer them cruel and unhinged, Jacques," Angelo spat back, bracing himself.

Sapphira's eyes, cold and calculating, met Angelo's. For a moment, something flickered in their depths - a hint of an old, unhealed wound.

"You look at me with such judgment, Angelo," she said, her voice a mixture of silk and steel. "Tell me, have you ever lost everything? Have you watched your world crumble, powerless to stop it?"

Without waiting for an answer, she continued, her gaze distant. "I had a daughter once, you know. Marguerite. She was everything to me - my light, my hope for a legacy that would outlast even our immortal lives."

Sapphira's hand clenched, her nails digging into her palm hard enough to draw blood. "But the world is cruel, especially to those who are different. A mob, fueled by fear and ignorance, took her from me. They called her a witch, a demon... they didn't understand the gift she had inherited."

Her eyes refocused on Angelo, blazing with a mixture of pain and fury. "I learned then that power is the only true protection. Compassion is a luxury we cannot afford. Every life I take, every rule I break - it's all to ensure that what happened to my Marguerite never happens again."

Jacques watched this exchange with a mix of surprise and satisfaction, clearly pleased to see this vulnerable side of his powerful progeny.

Angelo, despite his revulsion at Sapphira's actions, felt a pang of empathy. He understood loss, the way it could twist a person. But he also knew it was no excuse for the atrocities she had committed.

"Loss doesn't justify cruelty," Angelo said softly. "It should teach us compassion, not callousness."

Sapphira's laugh was bitter. "Compassion? Tell that to the mob that burned my daughter. No, Angelo. The world doesn't reward compassion. It rewards strength. And I intend to be the strongest of all."

The ancient vampire circled Angelo as mystical chains wrapped around him suddenly. "We could have ruled eternally, you and I. Instead, you betrayed our vision - chose to leash yourself to pathetic human morality." Jacques tightened his fist around Angelo's throat slowly, as Sapphira watched coolly from across the room, continuing her dark incantations over the captives. "Perhaps I shall remind you of the glorious freedom we once reveled in... after my dear Sapphira tends to your gory punishment first," Jacques smiled sinisterly. Angelo focused his fading mind on a desperate telepathic plea, before Marie's fury exploded into the cabin. As the women battled violently, Angelo managed to finally shatter his conjured bonds.

He turned to the unstable Sapphira, seeing her now not just as a monster, but as a broken soul twisted by grief. "You don't have to let his cruelty define you! I've helped others like you back from the shadows..."

At his words, something seemed to fracture in her. She clutched her head screaming, explosive energy erupting outward. Then she vanished instantly, leaving only scorched floor behind.

Alone later, shaken by the darkness in her eyes that he glimpsed in that last moment, Angelo knew this was far from over. Sapphira would return for him, more dangerous than ever... and now, tragically, he understood why. The hunt had just begun, but it was no longer just a chase for justice. It had become a race to save a soul from the abyss of its own making.

Chapter 4: Innocence Lost

Angelo is assaulted by a pervading sense of wrongness even blocks away from the new crime scene. As if ghostly wraiths of atrocities still tethered to restless living perpetrators brush against his speeding sleek vehicle flooding instincts with urgent dismay of brutal violations ahead.

As feared, multiple squad cars box in a dingy alley cordoned off from prying eyes. But the small, shrouded form between sorrowful officers crushes the breath from Angelo's heart instantly with crushing implications. The figure beside Clay making notes as he approaches is tragically, sickeningly child-sized...

Kneeling solemnly beside the small broken corpse, Angelo carefully turns over the child's wrist, bile rising to see bruises and ligature markings confirming clearly non-accidental tragedy. He blinks hard detecting faint elongated puncture outlines still discernible from Sapphira's unique triple-fanged jaw imprint haunting far too many cold case photos in confidential manila folders.

As Angelo straightened up, a familiar scent caught his attention – jasmine mixed with something... magical. He turned to find himself face to face with Andrea Deveraux, the local witch who sometimes consulted on particularly puzzling cases. Her green eyes met his, and for a moment, the rest of the world seemed to fade away.

"Detective Dubois," she greeted him, her voice carrying a hint of amusement. "Fancy meeting you here."

Angelo cleared his throat, suddenly aware of how close they were standing. "Ms. Deveraux. I didn't realize you'd been called in."

"I sensed the magical disturbance," she explained, tucking a strand of raven hair behind her ear. "Thought you might need some... expert assistance."

As she spoke, her hand brushed against Angelo's arm, and he felt a jolt of electricity at the contact. It was more than just the usual static spark – there was a definite magical undercurrent to it. He couldn't help but notice the way the moonlight caught in her hair, or the subtle scent of jasmine that seemed to surround her.

"Well," Angelo said, his voice a touch huskier than usual, "I certainly won't turn down expert help. What can you tell me about this scene?"

Andrea knelt beside the victim, her brow furrowing in concentration. As she worked, Angelo found himself watching her intently. He'd worked with her before, of course, but something felt different this time. There was an energy in the air between them, a tension that hadn't been there before.

"There's definitely dark magic at play here," Andrea murmured, her fingers hovering over the child's body without touching it. "It's... old. Powerful. And familiar." She looked up at Angelo, her eyes wide with concern. "This has Sapphira written all over it."

Marie's fingers traced an old scar on her wrist, a mark left by generations of magical lineage. "These are signatures I remember from the old stories," she muttered. "Techniques of the coastal covens, passed down from the early settlers - French, African, and Indigenous magic blending into something... uniquely Creole. Something with roots deeper than most understand.

Angelo nodded grimly. "My thoughts exactly. But why a child? It's not her usual M.O."

Andrea stood, brushing off her knees. "Maybe she's escalating. Or maybe..." She trailed off, her gaze distant.

"Maybe what?" Angelo prompted, stepping closer to her.

Andrea shook her head, as if clearing away cobwebs. "It's probably nothing. Just a wild theory."

"Hey," Angelo said softly, placing a hand on her shoulder. "Your wild theories have cracked cases before. What are you thinking?"

The moment his hand touched her shoulder, that spark flared again. Andrea's eyes met his, and for a second, it felt like the entire world held its breath. Then she blinked, and the moment passed.

"I'm thinking," she said slowly, "that this might be more than just a murder. It could be a ritual."

Angelo's brow furrowed. "A ritual? For what purpose?"

"To strengthen her power," Andrea explained. "There are... dark rituals that can use the life force of an innocent to bolster one's magical abilities. It's forbidden magic, of course, but if anyone would dare to use it..."

"It would be Sapphira," Angelo finished. He ran a hand through his hair, frustration evident in every line of his body. "Damn it. As if she wasn't powerful enough already."

Andrea placed a comforting hand on his arm. "We'll stop her, Angelo. We have to."

The use of his first name didn't escape Angelo's notice. It felt... right, somehow. Intimate in a way that sent a shiver down his spine.

Rage boils suddenly within Angelo and the very breeze stills unnaturally. Whirling up from his crouch, he unleashes a feral snarl into the shadows. "I know you lurk gleefully over this innocent's undeserved torment, hell spawn! Come face damnation your monstrosity holds long overdue!"

Only silence answers his raw challenge until wisps of jasmine and bone-chilling static herald Sapphira decloaking mere inches from Angelo's coiled fury. Smug defiance etches flawless features as she surveys the covered corpse almost tenderly to enflame his protectiveness further. "We reap...what we sow in my gardens, naive princeling. You spurn my generosity offering clarity on our true divine design without consequence?" One blood pearl fang glints as Sapphira's smile widens. "Then face such pathetic mewling fates multiplying upon your misguided mercy!"

She embraces the suspended moment, avarice drinking Angelo's anguish deeply. "Lead your deluded police puppets by leashes yet if you must. But each new innocent lamb I choose bleeding out will imprint this lesson ever deeper I vow, my sweet detective..." With a final caress of the small dead face between them, she vanishes on icy winds...leaving Angelo alone staring brokenly down once more at the boy who could be sleeping save for eternal closure his gaze shall never know.

As Sapphira vanished, Angelo felt a warm hand slip into his. He looked down to see Andrea standing beside him, her face a mask of determination.

"You're not alone in this," she said firmly. "We'll bring her to justice, together."

Angelo squeezed her hand gratefully, marveling at how perfectly it fit in his. "Thank you," he murmured.

As they stood there, united in their resolve, Angelo couldn't help but feel that something fundamental had shifted between them. This shared trauma, this mutual understanding of the darkness they faced, had forged a connection that went beyond mere professional courtesy.

The rest of the night passed in a blur of evidence collection and witness interviews. Through it all, Angelo was acutely aware of Andrea's presence. She moved through the crime scene with grace and purpose, her magical insights proving invaluable to the investigation.

As dawn approached, Angelo found Andrea standing alone at the edge of the crime scene, her face turned towards the lightening sky.

"Penny for your thoughts?" he asked, coming to stand beside her.

Andrea sighed, running a hand through her hair. "I'm just... trying to make sense of it all. How someone could do this to a child. How Sapphira can be so callous, so cruel."

"I've been asking myself the same questions for centuries," Angelo admitted. "Sometimes I think I'm no closer to an answer now than I was when I first turned."

Andrea turned to look at him, her eyes searching his face. "How do you do it? How do you keep fighting when the darkness seems so overwhelming?"

Angelo was quiet for a moment, considering her question. "I guess... I hold onto hope. Hope that we can make a difference, even if it's just in small ways. Hope that there's still good in the world, worth protecting."

As he spoke, he found himself drawing closer to Andrea, as if pulled by an invisible force. She didn't back away, her gaze still locked with his.

"And now?" she asked softly. "What gives you hope now?"

Angelo's hand came up to cup her cheek, almost of its own accord. "You do," he whispered.

For a heartbeat, the world stood still. Then, slowly, inevitably, they leaned towards each other. Their lips met in a soft, tentative kiss that quickly deepened, filled with all the emotion and tension that had been building between them.

When they finally pulled apart, both were slightly breathless. Andrea's cheeks were flushed, her eyes bright with a mixture of surprise and something deeper, more profound.

"Well," she said, a small smile playing on her lips. "That was..."

"Unexpected?" Angelo supplied, his own smile mirroring hers.

"I was going to say 'about time'," Andrea replied, her smile widening.

Before Angelo could respond, they were interrupted by the arrival of Captain Rhemann. As they turned to face him, Angelo felt Andrea's hand slip into his once more. Whatever challenges lay ahead, whatever darkness Sapphira might throw at them, they would face it together.

The sun rose over New Orleans, painting the sky in hues of pink and gold. As Angelo and Andrea walked back to the crime scene, hand in hand, they knew that their fight against Sapphira was far from over. But now, they had something new to fight for – not just justice, not just the protection of the innocent, but a future together, a beacon of light in the darkness that threatened to engulf their city.

Chapter 5: Confrontation in the projects

The acrid smell of gunpowder mingled with fresh blood, assaulting Angelo's senses as he stepped into the chaos of the drive-by shooting on Canal Street. Keen vision sweeping over the chaos, at first, he spotted nothing overtly supernatural that street cops would miss. But a faint iron-laced scent down a deserted alley tickled his memory. He followed it through a broken basement window gaping open behind a jazz lounge facade. Faint blood droplets formed a telling trail - not human essence, but corrupted vampire energy instead. The clues led back to one dangerous perpetrator after all...Sapphira. The unique blood markers ultimately led Angelo to a notorious housing project blocks away. He traced faint smears upstairs to a dented apartment door, loud music and video games blaring within.

Inside, Angelo found the teenage shooter frozen in surprise on the sagging couch. "Little late for Kill zone, ain't its kid?" Angelo said, blurring vampire-quick to pin the gang banger by the throat before he could reach any weapons. "Whatchu want, old fang? You ain't got no badge to push up in here!" The trapped teenager defiantly jutted his chin despite choking panic. Angelo tightened his vice-like grip, eyes burning icy fire now.

"Your boss and I have unfinished business. And you're going to take me to her."

But Sapphira herself suddenly manifested from the darkened threshold, slow clapping. "Oh, do be gentle with my new help, Angelo dear...good, hired fangs are ever so hard to come by since you started scaring them off."

As Angelo examined the blood trail, Captain Rhemann appeared suddenly beside him. "Nasty business, this," Rhemann muttered, then gestured to the uniformed officers. "Boys, give Detective Dubois some space. This is... sensitive." Once alone, Rhemann spoke softly. "You might want to wrap this up quickly, Dubois. Some evidence doesn't hold up well in the light of day, if you catch my drift." Angelo watched his captain walk away, suspicion growing. Despite her flippant tone, Angelo detected something fractured beneath Sapphira's surface as she surveyed the carelessly bleeding teen. She seemed disturbed by unnecessary weakness used and discarded. He changed tack - appealing not to her violent foot soldier, but the broken mistress behind the chaos.

"There's always been blood on both our hands, Sapphira. But once I fed without discretion or mercy under no banners, but selfish impulse passed off as mere nature," Angelo confessed. "What makes either of us spare some lives now when we could so easily erase all?" A sneer flickered across her haughty features at the thinly veiled criticism of her moral code's absence. She viciously ripped away the teen's bloodied towel, tracing one claw lightly as he whimpered. "Mercy? Morality? Those are but mortal myths vampires fool themselves with so they can pretend there are still human souls inside," she scoffed. "Why curb our hunger? We are apex predators, divine!"

She grasped the semi-conscious teenager's head, neck stretched painfully. "When you could gorge eternally on gods' nectar as is our birthright..." Angelo swallowed hard, shamefully remembering his earlier alleyway slaughter. Perhaps she was right about his fractured nature...

Sapphira clearly resented Angelo's ongoing selective morality. "You prowl dispensing 'justice' between feedings, choosing who lives or dies by some quaint moral compass?" She slammed the teen's body down, bored. "If you insist on defending sheep, guardian wolf, then I may just have to slay you too." Sapphira moved closer, grasp firm on Angelo's chin to remind him of her enduring power as New Orleans' true vampire ruler. "This city flows with blood by my rule. You'd do well attuned to that, always."

Resentment simmered in Angelo. But even in the throes of wounded ego, he knew he could no more reclaim firm standing across her ruthless dominion than tear its fabric apart. At least not yet...

As Angelo turned to retreat temporarily, Sapphira revealed she had glamoured his police captain years ago, securing Angelo's badge as disguise to serve her. "Fail to offer fitting tithes before the next full moon...and no backroom deal will shield what scraps remain."

She vanished with a rustle of shadows...but the warning etched bone deep. A dangerous hunt lay ahead.

Chapter 6: The Weight of Centuries

Centuries of buried memories crashed over Angelo like a tidal wave, drowning out the wail of approaching sirens. He glimpsed his younger self clutching his anxious mother's palm the muggy night his father insisted on paying call to the notorious Sapphira LeCroix.

Her blood-soaked legacy and iron rule intimidated all regional vampires, yet the Dubois sought her blessing.

Inside the ramshackle Creole townhouse, young Angelo shuddered under Sapphira's invasive inspection. Though the host wore an immaculate French lace dress, she exuded power eclipsing her vessel. Strange violet tattoos swirled up her bare arms, hinting at ancient, unleashed forces enslaving generations.

"To what do I owe this... pleasure, Monsieur Dubois?" Sapphira purred indulgently. But her heavy stare quickly turned raptorial noticing timid young Angelo. "And you finally bring the next Dubois heir before me. Thirteen years overdue for my assessment..."

Angelo's father bowed stiffly beside his trembling son. "The boy must now learn governance binding our hidden circles. And who safeguards those systems here to mutual benefit." It sounded like well-rehearsed sycophancy. With a negligent wave, grandeur engulfed the decaying parlor. Sapphira pointed with haughty pride to an imposing family crest now adorning the marble hearth as she held court.

Angelo noticed several imposing figures lingering in the shadows beyond the parlor, their stillness almost supernatural. Sapphira caught his curious gaze. 'The Elder Council observes, young one,' she whispered with cold amusement. 'They govern our kind when even I must bend to ancient law. Remember their eyes upon you always.' A chill ran down Angelo's spine as unseen gazes weighed his worth from the darkness.

"Was it not I who catapulted your grandsire from petty smuggler to shipping tycoon against Texan aggressions?" Past visions of vast mercantile success bled through before she dismissed them impatiently. "And did your father does not pledge me covert profits from his medical aspirations?" Angelo's father shrank under reminder of their binding, oaths sworn for enterprise ascent. This creature selected citywide fates on her passing whims. Sapphira's eyes took on a distant look, as if seeing beyond the confines of the room and into the vast expanse of her own history. "You wonder, don't you, child?" she addressed young Angelo directly, her voice taking on an almost hypnotic quality. "You wonder how one such as I came to be."

The room seemed to darken, the candlelight flickering as if buffeted by an unseen wind. Angelo's parents exchanged nervous glances but remained silent as Sapphira continued.

"I was born in a time of fire and blood," she said, her eyes gleaming with memories. "The year was 1095, and the First Crusade had just begun. I was a noblewoman's daughter, destined for a life of luxury and arranged marriages." Her laugh was bitter, echoing through the room. "Fate, it seems, had other plans. Our castle was sacked, my family slaughtered. I alone survived, hidden away by a servant who saw... potential in me."

Young Angelo listened, transfixed, as Sapphira wove her tale. She spoke of a vampire elder who took her in, who saw in her a ruthlessness born of survival. She described centuries of learning, of clawing her way to power in a world that sought to use and discard her. "I swore then," Sapphira said, her voice dropping to a whisper that somehow filled the room, "that I would never be powerless again. That I would build a kingdom where our kind could thrive, safe from the petty whims of mortals and their endless wars." Her eyes refocused on Angelo, sharp and predatory. "Do you understand now, child? Why I do what I must? Why I demand absolute loyalty?"

Young Angelo, despite his fear, found himself nodding. He could see the pain behind her eyes, the weight of centuries pressing down on her.

Sapphira's expression softened, just for a moment. "Good. Remember this lesson well, young Dubois. Power protects. Power preserves. And I will do whatever it takes to ensure our survival."

With a wave of her hand, the oppressive atmosphere lifted. Sapphira turned back to Angelo's parents, all business once more. "Now, as for your place in my vision..." As the memory faded, adult Angelo found himself back in the present, the echo of sirens fading into the distance. He understood now, more than ever, the complexity of the monster they faced. Sapphira wasn't just a tyrant drunk on power. She was a survivor, shaped by centuries of hardship and loss, convinced that her iron rule was the only thing standing between their kind and annihilation.

It didn't excuse her actions, the lives she'd ruined, the innocents she'd sacrificed. But it made her more than a simple villain to be vanquished. She was a product of her time, of her experiences, of the harsh world that had forged her.

Angelo sighed heavily, the weight of this knowledge settling on his shoulders. Defeating Sapphira wouldn't just be a matter of overpowering her. They would need to prove her wrong. To show that there was another way, a better way, to protect their kind without resorting to tyranny.

As he stepped out into the night, ready to face whatever new crisis awaited, Angelo steeled himself for the battles to come. Not just the physical confrontations, but the ideological war that lay at the heart of their conflict. It would be a long, hard road ahead, but one he was now more prepared than ever to walk.

Chapter 7: A grizzly discovery

Dawn's purple fingers clawed at the sky as Angelo slunk back to the precinct, his hunt for Sapphira's phantoms leaving him drained in many ways. Her scattered blood essential fragments always dead-ended before any conclusive truths emerged. Inside, Angelo nearly collided with fellow detective Washington barreling downstairs, thoroughly jacked on midnight caffeine. "We caught a scene needs your weird mojo ASAP, Dubois!" Washington exclaimed. "Whoa slow down, Wash. What we looking at?" Angelo grasped the frenzied man's shoulders. "Councilman's wild child daughter Lisa Albrecht - got herself murdered tonight!" the lieutenant filled in. "Workers spotted her body dumped behind warehouses at the wharfs just before sunrise."

As the first rays of dawn began to creep over the horizon, Angelo felt the familiar tingle in his skin. He reached into his pocket, running his fingers over the smooth surface of his lapis lazuli ring. The ancient piece of jewelry, a Dubois family heirloom, was more than just a trinket. Infused with powerful magic by a witch ancestor generations ago, it granted Angelo a rare gift among vampires - the ability to walk in daylight.

He slipped the ring onto his finger, feeling the magic pulse through him. It wasn't perfect protection; extended exposure to direct sunlight could still weaken him, and he'd never be comfortable in the midday sun. But it allowed him to move freely in the mortal world, to do his job as a detective without arousing suspicion.

Angelo smiled wryly to himself. The ring was both a blessing and a curse. It set him apart from other vampires, making him an oddity in their nocturnal society. But it also gave him a freedom that few of his kind could ever dream of. As he stepped out into the early morning light, he silently thanked his ancestors for their foresight.

Angelo instinctively scented old blood, but no lingering vampiric notes reached his attuned senses in the harbor breeze. He knew Lisa's salacious reputation well enough. "We sure it's her for real?"

"Those crazy society gal pals ID'd her fast enough once curls and diamond tennis bracelets met light," Washington replied cynically as they raced toward flashing patrol lights in the distance, glad for violence beyond Sapphira's usual artful spectacle. The lead detective soon intercepted them, steering Angelo away from the bustling crime scene. "You look like nine kinds of hell. Let the humans run lab tests while you grab some solid rack time." He nodded towards the brightening horizon. Reluctantly Angelo obeyed, descending into concealing sewer access tunnels making his lightproof trek home. As Angelo descended into the sewer tunnels, he moved with an ease belying the popular misconception that all vampires must flee daylight's exposure. In addition to the ring, a rare bloodline adaptation granted him resilience against the sun's harsh rays where most kindred would swiftly combust.

Angelo was thus able pass undetected working normal shift hours alongside the mortal detectives. While they praise his uncanny knack for nocturnal cases, not one has the faintest clue their star colleague's undead nature empowering such effective dark prowls.

Angelo shifted a concealing sewer hole cover at street level cautiously. Peering out reveals ordinary crowds bustling under a bright autumn morning, unaware of paranormal predators concealed amongst them. He checked his antique lapis lazuli ring, the enchanted stone facilitating his special day-walking protection ever since that fateful 18th birthday when it surfaced amongst other inherited Dubois heirlooms.

Its steadfast magic cloaked Angelo in sufficient mortal facade for short periods when needed. Like now, exiting the tunnels to hail a taxi in front of unsuspecting commuters. While the ring didn't permit full immunity forever outside vampire realms, it granted adequate daylight privileges without betraying his true monstrous essence. At least for a while longer on this brisk dawn...before appetites and exhaustion drive the detective back into concealing darkness until night descends once more over New Orleans. Safely inside, Angelo loosens his concealing lapis lazuli ring sustaining resilience against daylight's harsh exposure where other vampires would swiftly combust. The enchanted heirloom facilitates his working alongside oblivious mortal partners by cloaking undead nature. Its magic could grant no permanent immunity but offered adequate privilege to work before night's sheltering darkness descended over New Orleans once more.

Angelo froze as he flicked on the light, realizing Sapphira had clearly been lying in wait for him within the shadows of his cramped apartment's entryway. Her sudden presence teased connection to the unsolved murder Lt. Mackey had updated him on back at the precinct. "Fancy meeting you here, my wayward stray from the coven..." Sapphira said with a mirthless smirk. "However, do you tolerate such squalor as home? Much less focus on the blood trails I plant like gosling feed when your decor would drive out rats themselves?"

Ignoring her mocking jabs, Angelo crossed his arms warily. "I have a feeling you didn't drop by unannounced to critique my living situation. What did you do to that Albrecht girl they dragged from the harbor, Sapphira?" The ancient vampiress glided to Angelo's cluttered desk, fingering curled crime scene snapshots as if searching for her likeness amongst the victims catalogued there over decades. "So, the council elite are harmed, and heaven's lead defender finally takes notice? When street creatures have fallen prey to our court's indulgence for centuries..."

Sapphira sighed in disgust. "Make no mistake, little prince. Lisa Albrecht was no innocent babe left to slum for wayward thrills." Her fiery glare suggested heavy implications. "She made certain beds, now she's merely resting eternally in them. Case. Closed."

Angelo digested her words carefully, intuiting there are hidden context clues possibly influencing the investigation. But Sapphira's presence confirmed his worst fear - that the councilman's lost daughter may have been directly targeted and her body strategically dumped to mock human justice limitations...and Angelo's own.

Chapter 8: Sunrise and secrets

The sun's unflinching gaze seared the retreating night shadows as Angelo slid his ancient family ring onto his finger - masking lethal vampire essence to withstand daylight for short periods. A deception allowing him to masquerade as human for centuries amidst New Orleans's raucous mortal chaos and brutal crime scenes as lead homicide detective. But that hard-won control would be tested this cycle. Sliding behind the wheel of his blacked-out muscle car before most day walkers stirred, Sapphira herself manifested in the passenger seat out of thin air, her evergreen and jasmine perfume cutting through residual blood scents. Piercing onyx eyes roved over Angelo. "Still obstinately clinging to that ridiculous policeman fantasy I see. Pretending at humanity under that gaudy Gothic mood ring's greater magical mercy. Have I not leveled punishment enough over the long burning decades for your defiance?" Sapphira drawled dangerously, one elegant claw flicking the lapis lazuli sigil in disgust.

Angelo's grip tightened on the leather=wrapped steering wheel, jaw clenched. "I walk in shadows or light by choice and conscience now, not your personal whim. And protect the vulnerable from more than just predators of our supernatural kind." Sapphira's sudden lilting laugh echoed through the sunlit car. "We shall see how well stubborn pride preserves against chaos unleashed on your quaint mortal dynasty this night, my fallen avenger..." Before Angelo could demand explanation for the ominous taunt, Sapphira dissolved into vine-choked mist. Uneasy already, he sped towards the station to find a female jogger's violently mutilated corpse had been dumped deep in outlying park woods. Gazing at the macabre scene, he noted the same brutal force that claimed a vagrant dockworker the week before - likely part of some dark spree.

Detective McLeod surveyed the bloodied vegetation frowning. "Another long cold case for the boards until we catch our specified flavor of sicko." The veteran homicide chief pointed to several small, removed fingers already bagged for CSI. "Takes a real creative demon to carve body parts off out here like freakin reagents..." The old Scot turned hawk-eyed noting his colleague sniff subtly as if following phantom scent trails. "You got that uncanny bloodhound vibe just like at the wharf site, Dubois?" He arched one wiry grey brow. "Should put in for transfer to new K9 patrol unit at this rate."

Angelo straightened quickly from where he hovered over faint crushed foliage. "Just surveying all possibilities as you always say to, boss." He flashed a disarming grin that didn't reach weary eyes before striding back to the heart of the bustling forensic activity. Away from sidelong peers, Angelo conceded McLeod had reason for suspicion. Beneath iron-laced adrenaline and fear sharp as cut glass from the victim, familiar cruel orchestration indeed teased his senses. Sapphira was already moving her next pawn in this deadly game between them, mutilations a taunting message she knew he would recognize.

Chapter 9: Whispers in the Dark Wave

The inky darkness of the New Orleans night enveloped the city, broken only by the flickering neon signs and the soft glow of gas lamps lining the streets of the French Quarter. Angelo Dubois, his vampiric senses on high alert, made his way through the labyrinthine alleys towards the discreet dark wave bistro off the French Quarter. The weight of recent events hung heavy on his shoulders, each step a reminder of the dangers that lurked in the shadows of the city he'd sworn to protect.

As he approached the bistro, the familiar scent of black orchid and night-blooming jasmine teased his heightened senses. A small smile tugged at the corner of his lips, his tension easing slightly at the knowledge that Andrea was already there. Their relationship had grown from reluctant allies to trusted partners, and now to something deeper, more profound. It was a development that both thrilled and terrified him, given the dangerous world they inhabited.

The soft click of stiletto heels on polished stone announced Andrea's arrival seconds before Angelo saw her. She materialized across from him, her raven pixie cut framing intelligent green eyes that seemed to pierce right through him. The black leather dress she wore clung to dangerous curves, a stark contrast to the delicate floral scents that always seemed to surround her.

"You're late," Andrea said, a hint of amusement in her voice as she slid into the booth opposite Angelo.

He raised an eyebrow, a smirk playing on his lips. "A wizard is never late, nor is he early. He arrives precisely when he means to."

Andrea rolled her eyes, but her smile widened. "Are you quoting Gandalf at me, Detective? I didn't realize you were such a nerd."

"There's a lot you don't know about me," Angelo replied, his tone light but his eyes serious.

A moment of charged silence passed between them, filled with unspoken words and shared memories. Andrea broke it first, reaching across the table to place her hand on Angelo's wrist. Her thumb traced the nearly faded punctures from his recent struggles, her touch gentle but firm.

"Rough night upholding justice, I see," she murmured, her eyes searching his face for signs of distress.

Angelo sighed, the weariness he'd been holding at bay suddenly crashing over him. "You could say that. Sometimes I wonder if we're making any difference at all."

Andrea's grip on his wrist tightened slightly. "Hey, none of that. You're doing important work, Angelo. We both are."

He nodded, grateful for her unwavering support. It was one of the things he loved most about her – her ability to ground him, to remind him of their purpose when the weight of their responsibilities threatened to overwhelm him.

"You're right," he conceded. "It's just... these streets grow more blood-drenched by the night, my love." He exhaled heavily, allowing some of his carefully constructed walls to crumble in her presence. "The police force struggles curtailing ordinary violence outbreaks from gang wars lately ... now arcane impropriety taints the mix as well, thanks to that estranged clan elder of ours behind curtained scenes."

Andrea squeezed his hand supportively, her eyes flashing with a mixture of concern and determination. "We'll figure it out, Angelo. We always do."

Their conversation was interrupted by the arrival of their usual server, a young vampire named Lila who had a knack for discretion. She set down two glasses of a deep red liquid that Angelo knew wasn't wine, at least not in the traditional sense.

As they sipped their drinks, Angelo found himself studying Andrea's face, marveling at the play of candlelight across her features. He remembered the first time they'd met, how he'd dismissed her as just another witch dabbling in matters beyond her understanding. How wrong he'd been.

"What are you thinking about?" Andrea asked, catching his gaze.

"The first time we worked a case together," Angelo admitted. "Remember that haunted jazz club on Frenchmen Street?"

Andrea laughed, the sound like music to Angelo's ears. "How could I forget? You were so sure you could handle it on your own. And then that possessed saxophone nearly took your head off."

"If you hadn't been there with that binding spell..." Angelo shook his head, chuckling at the memory.

"We make a good team," Andrea said softly, her eyes meeting his over the rim of her glass.

The air between them seemed to crackle with unspoken emotion. Angelo found himself leaning forward, drawn in by the warmth in Andrea's gaze. But before he could close the distance, a loud crash from the kitchen shattered the moment.

Both of them were on their feet in an instant, bodies tense and ready for action. But it was just a busboy who had dropped a tray of glasses, not the supernatural threat they'd both instinctively prepared for.

As they settled back into their seats, Angelo couldn't help but laugh. "We're a bit on edge, aren't we?"

Andrea smiled ruefully. "Comes with the territory, I suppose. Speaking of which..." Her expression grew serious. "There's something I need to tell you about Sapphira."

Angelo felt a chill run down his spine at the mention of the vampire queen's name. He knew mentioning her, even obliquely, risked dangerous emotional territory given Andrea's mysterious family background tying her to the volatile vampiress' sprawling influence throughout New Orleans.

"What is it?" he asked, his voice low and urgent.

Andrea took a deep breath, her fingers toying restlessly with the antique serpent armband coiled around her creamy shoulder. "I've heard whispers... rumors of dissension within her court. Some of the younger vampires are growing restless under her rule."

Angelo leaned in closer, his mind already racing with the implications. "Do you think there could be a coup?"

"It's possible," Andrea replied, her voice barely above a whisper. "But Sapphira's not one to give up power easily. If she even suspects disloyalty..."

The unspoken threat hung in the air between them. They both knew all too well the brutality Sapphira was capable of.

"We need to be careful," Angelo said, his jaw set with determination. "If there's going to be a power struggle, we need to be prepared. The last thing this city needs is an all-out vampire war."

Andrea nodded, her expression mirroring his resolve. "I'll reach out to my contacts in the witch community. See if we can gather more information."

As the night wore on, they continued to strategize, their heads bent close together over the table. To anyone watching, they might have looked like any other couple enjoying a late-night drink. But the fate of New Orleans hung in the balance of their whispered conversation.

Finally, as the first hints of dawn began to lighten the sky, they prepared to leave. Angelo helped Andrea into her coat, his hand lingering on her shoulder.

"Be careful," he murmured, his eyes searching hers. "I couldn't bear it if anything happened to you."

Andrea reached up, cupping his cheek gently. "I'm always careful. And I've got you watching my back, don't I?"

Angelo nodded, covering her hand with his own. For a moment, they stood there, lost in each other's gaze. Then, with a shared smile and a final squeeze of hands, they parted ways, each disappearing into the awakening city.

As Angelo made his way home, he couldn't shake the feeling that they were standing on the precipice of something monumental. But with Andrea by his side, he felt ready to face whatever challenges lay ahead. Together, they would protect their city, no matter the cost.

Chapter 10: Clash in the Flower Shop

Andrea hummed softly, deftly weaving night-blooming jasmine and orchids into stunning arrangements for the customer procession through her cozy French Quarter floral boutique. Despite haunting family trauma unearthed recently, losing herself amidst fragrant therapy and smiling patrons flowed restorative as blood itself.

A sudden frigid gust extinguished every candle plunging the room mute and dim. Before the startled gasp left Andrea's throat, Sapphira materialized inches away glowering with palpable malevolence. Frozen mid-transaction, human shoppers stand helpless as Winter herself prowls silently nearer shadowing Springtime Andrea threateningly.

"Rather quaint digs suit a tamed house-cat more than an alpha predator." Sapphira sniffed disdainfully scanning the vibrant displays. "But I suppose playacting shepherdess soothes past injuries my ineffective guardianship invited upon your rather...unique mortal breed."

Andrea refused to flinch under barbed words, mercurial fury rising to match the necromantic chill infusing her haven. This obstinate hell beast dared besmirch her hard-won peaceful sanctuary.

"At least this 'shepherdess' thrives independently without hoarding lives to validate power." Andrea boldly met ancient eyes, magic against magic and will against will. "What excuse grants violating my sovereign turf unannounced, Auntie?"

She spat the familial address like poison darts.

Sapphira's onyx eyes flared dangerously hearing bitter blood bonds invoked so brazenly. "Mind yourself, niece, I brook no disrespect even from last vestiges of witch blood too tainted for my protection centuries before."

She manifested suddenly inches behind a frozen elderly patron, one blood red claw trailing his fragile neck. "As the apex Creole elder and appointed immortal steward since Antoinette Leclerc's dynasty collapsed, all domains throughout New Orleans fall under my jurisdiction...ill-begotten upstart kin claiming Southern witch heritage or no."

The temperature plunged further in Andrea's blood, but she refused the bait of endangering the helpless mortal. "Yet never have I or mine seen Sanctuary Rights honored after paying steep tithes your umbrella demands." Andrea moved cautiously between Sapphira and her paralyzed patrons. "Where was vaunted Elder aid when Papist executors bound my sister in unholy iron? When hundreds cried for mercy upon Creole soil?"

Rage ignition within Andrea began manifesting protective runes shimmering to life along the suddenly restored floral walls. "Your authority wanes thin as veiled threats when innocents required safe harbor behind that ostentatious crown, Auntie..."

Seeing Andrea openly dare challenge her prestige fanned Sapphira's fury. "Uppity cur mixbloods - I should have left your whimpering lot to hunters' hallowed mercy blades!"

In a flash, her claws were suddenly snared by thorny rose vines bursting up through floorboards. Andrea focused crackling violet energy down the writhing conduit around Sapphira's shocked wrist.

"The only whimpering cur I see skulks shackled before me now...nobility and ruthlessness make for piss poor saviors when authentic hearts demanded your grace." Andrea cockily tracked a single blood droplet down Sapphira's wrist.

Just as the confrontation reached its peak, the shop's door bursts open. Angelo rushed in, his eyes wild with concern.

"Andrea!" he called out, taking in the scene before him.

Sapphira's lips curl into a cruel smile. "Ah, the knight arrives to save his witch. How quaint."

Angelo moved to Andrea's side, his hand brushing against hers. Even in the midst of danger, that simple touch sent a jolt of electricity through them both.

"I don't need saving," Andrea said, her voice steady despite the flush creeping up her neck. "But I appreciate the backup."

Together, they face Sapphira, their combined auras creating a palpable force in the small shop. The air crackles with tension - both from the confrontation and the unspoken attraction between Angelo and Andrea.

Sapphira's eyes narrowed as she observed their united front. "How touching," she sneers. "The vampire and the witch, thinking they can defy the natural order."

"There's nothing unnatural about this," Angelo growled, stepping slightly in front of Andrea protectively.

Andrea placed a hand on Angelo's arm, the gesture intimate and reassuring. "We're stronger together," she declared, her eyes never leaving Sapphira's face.

The ancient vampire's face contorted with rage. "You fool!" she spat at Angelo. "You would choose this... this witch over your own kind?"

"Every time," Angelo replied without hesitation.

Sapphira unleashed a wave of dark energy, but Andrea and Angelo stand firm, their powers intertwining to create a shield. As they pushed back against Sapphira's assault, they find themselves pressed close together, acutely aware of each other's presence.

"Why my flawed ward exceeds your vaunted station serving vulnerable dying breaths more earnestly each week than a thousand entitled council sessions - " Andrea began, but Sapphira cut her off with a scream of banshee outrage.

Sapphira channeled unholy darkness towards Andrea's insolent smug face...desperate to reassert unquestioned dominion before key players doubted much further...

The air itself ignited with ancient power awaiting release...

The miasma faded instantly along with Andrea's formidable power leaving only the heady aroma of her witch orchids lingering once more. She blinked rapidly, suddenly unsteady surveying damage throughout the quaint boutique from their apocalyptic grudge match unconsciously waged. Stunned to reassert composure, she started reshelving herbal materials.

Until implications behind Sapphira's parting threat against her beloved detective was truly processed...along with dread realizing vulnerabilities that were exposed before merciless fangs poised to tear apart their hard-won lives together.

As the last echoes of Sapphira's threats faded, Angelo turned to Andrea, his eyes roving over her to check for injuries. "Are you all right?" he asked, his voice husky with concern and lingering adrenaline.

Andrea nodded, suddenly very aware of how close they are standing. "I'm fine," she breathed, her eyes locked with his.

For a moment, they stood there, the air between them charged with unspoken emotions. Angelo's hand came up to cup Andrea's cheek, his thumb gently tracing her cheekbone.

"Andrea, I-" he began, but was cut off by the sound of sirens approaching.

They stepped apart reluctantly, the moment broken but the tension still simmering between them.

"We should clean up," Andrea says, gesturing to the chaos around them. "Before the police arrive."

Angelo nodded, but his eyes never left Andrea's face. As they worked to restore order to the shop, stolen glances and lingering touches spoke volumes about the feelings they are both struggling to contain.

The battle with Sapphira was far from over, but a new, equally powerful force was growing between them - one that will shape their fates in ways they have yet to imagine.

Chapter 11: The Summons

The Versailles Mausoleum loomed before Andrea, its weathered stone steps shrouded in ethereal mist. As she approached the moss-draped gates, a shiver ran down her spine. This was where the supreme New Orleans witch council judged blood matters, and tonight, she had been summoned.

Andrea's sleek Jaguar pulled up to the abandoned mausoleum, its engine purring to a stop. The iron tang of powerful witch magic hung in the air, mingling with the chill of death. This accursed den of familial corpses and coven secrets was the last place she wanted to be, but Sapphira's summons could not be ignored. The creaking iron entrance yielded to her touch, cool damp air rushing out to greet her. Flickering candlelight illuminated the worn stone halls, lined with the weathered tombs of Salem and French Quarter lords. Andrea's footsteps echoed in the silence as she made her way to the tall arched double doors, where ornate script etched into the lintel read:

ONLY THE HALLOWED AND THE DAMNED MAY ENTER

Beyond those doors waited Sapphira LeCroix, mistress of a thousand blood tides and Andrea's eternal enemy. Swallowing hard, Andrea whispered a prayer and pushed the doors open. The cloying scent of incense couldn't mask Sapphira's distinctive iron and jasmine perfume. The vampire queen stood imperiously at the head of a long oaken table, carved with forgotten druid protection spells. Surrounding her were the three ancients of the apex circle: bat-winged Vara, withered Sister Celine, and hollow-eyed Baron Dumar. As Andrea took her seat, Sapphira's cold gaze swept over her. "How kind of you to grace us with your presence, niece," she said, her voice dripping with sarcasm.

Andrea met her eyes steadily. "I came as summoned, Aunt. Though I confess, I'm curious about the urgency of this gathering." Sapphira's lips curled into a cruel smile. "All in good time, my dear. All in good time."

The vampire queen tapped her fingernails on the table, calling the unholy conclave to order. The other elders settled into an uneasy silence.

"I have called this urgent midnight tribunal," Sapphira began, her voice cutting through the tension, "because a cancer will spread unchecked, consuming our hallowed community from the inside."

She slammed down ancient scrolls, making Sister Celine jump. "A wayward neonate upstart calling himself Angelo Dubois has forsaken fealty and code that defines our proud lineage's noble continuity in New Orleans for centuries past!"

Baron Dumar leaned forward, his hollow eyes glinting with interest. "This Dubois... he's the vampire detective, is he not? I've heard whispers of his... unorthodox methods." Sapphira nodded curtly. "Indeed. And those methods threaten everything we've built." Her eyes blazed with fury as she continued, "The rabble feed unchecked, humans capitalize on fortunes, dismissing our sovereign foundations, because this... novel rogue detective playacts false sympathy, letting them!"

Vara hissed, her bat-like wings rustling. "Outrageous! He must be dealt with at once!"

"Precisely," Sapphira said, a triumphant gleam in her eye. "I move for immediate excommunication, revoking Dubois' privileged bloodline protections before he erodes fear and order completely!"

Her molten glare fixed on Andrea, challenging her to object. The room fell silent, the weight of centuries pressing down on them all.

It was Lenore, Sapphira's enigmatic second-in-command, who broke the silence. The ancient Seer lowered her feathered fan, revealing her ageless face. "Perhaps," she said softly, "we are being too hasty in our judgment." Sapphira's head snapped towards her. "Explain yourself, Lenore."

Lenore's azure eyes swept the room before settling on Sapphira. "This Angelo... violates no statutes outright warranting harshest separation sentence or outright execution decree," she began cautiously. "He merely conducts a peculiar experiment aligned with a curious conscience."

Sapphira scoffed. "Curious conscience? He's a threat to our very way of life!"

But Lenore continued, unperturbed. "If his unorthodox moral code proves a threat, then the option remains to adjust the experiment itself... through isolation and proper mentoring guidance. A far kinder remedy, I think, than permanence rendered so hastily."

The room erupted in murmurs, some of outrage, others of consideration.

"Kindness?" Vara spat. "Since when do we concern ourselves with kindness to traitors?"

Sister Celine, however, looked thoughtful. "Lenore may have a point. Our laws have always allowed for redemption..." Andrea, sensing her moment, rose to her feet. All eyes turned to her as she prepared to make her stand for Angelo's life. "If I may speak," she said, her voice steady despite her racing heart. Sapphira's eyes narrowed, but she nodded. "By all means, niece. Let's hear what defense you can muster for your... friend."

Chapter 12: The Decision

A nervous Andrea's voice rang clear through the chamber, silencing the murmurs. "There exist alternatives short of unjust slaughter for one whose sole crime shines light on how far our values have diverged from their true compass." She met each elder's gaze in turn, her words carefully chosen. "Rendering permanent judgment against this man also pronounces hypocrisy on our already cynical values. His lone trespass exposes how far astray our noble community charter has veered into oppression." Vara bristled. "How dare you accuse us of hypocrisy, child?"

"I dare because it's the truth," Andrea replied firmly. "Where stand our defining principles of sanctuary and discretion when feeds spill so carelessly, risking overexposure and drawing dangerous hunters back to our doors? Where hides wisdom and mercy while innocents are slaughtered weekly as petty object lessons?"

Her eyes locked with Sapphira's, unflinching. "My ladies, if Angelo Dubois warrants death simply for questioning the dysfunction festering within our order, then whatever meaning integrity once held has already expired in these chambers."

A tense silence followed her words. Even Sapphira seemed momentarily taken aback by Andrea's boldness. Lenore's eyes gleamed with approval from behind her fan.

"You speak of integrity," Sapphira said slowly, "but what of loyalty? What of the ancient laws that have kept our kind safe for centuries?" Andrea didn't back down. "Laws that no longer serve justice are not worthy of our loyalty. We must evolve, or we will perish." "Thus," Andrea concluded, her voice softening, "I say true justice lies in sparing one whose singular fault may be holding our judgments before a worthier mirror image too long denied. I move that the accused be shown community grace through isolation and retraining instead. The worthy path blazes light always on inner dark roads restored." As Andrea's final words echoed through the chamber, the heavy silence persisted. The elders exchanged glances, some thoughtful, others skeptical.

Sister Celine was the first to speak. "You've given us much to consider, child. Perhaps there is wisdom in your words." Baron Dumar nodded slowly. "It has been... some time since we've truly examined our ways. Perhaps this Dubois situation offers an opportunity for reflection."

Sapphira's face remained an impassive mask, but her eyes glittered dangerously. Finally, she spoke, her voice cutting through the tension. "You speak prettily, Andrea. But words alone cannot undo the damage your... friend has caused." She turned to address the council at large. "We have heard the arguments. Now, we must decide." The chamber crackled with nervous energy as Sapphira called for the vote. "We will proceed with the traditional clockwise voting order," she announced, her voice dripping with barely contained anger. She gestured to the first elder. "Baron Dumar, on the matter of Angelo Dubois the deviant, what say thee?" Andrea held her breath, her claws digging into her palms as she waited for the cadaverous nobleman's response. The Baron's hollow eyes seemed to look through them all as he pondered his decision. "Abstain," he rasped finally. "On grounds of inadequate evidence presented to merit a destroy decree this session. The case merits further review."

Andrea's claws dug furrows unconsciously under the table. The useless noncommittal position neither spared nor condemned Angelo. Everything now rode on the whims of the two Salem legacies left.

"Reverend Mother Celia," Sapphira intoned, "you stand longest in our traditions. Please render moral verdict over this breakaway apostate." The former nun's thin, withered lips parted slowly. "The rogue must reap wrathful justice sown. Sentence of death for Angelo Dubois the heretic." Andrea swallowed hard, despair threatening to overwhelm her. Ancient Egyptian Vara cackled in glee, already tallying the likely execution outcome. Only Lenore the Seer remained. But with no sway vote left possible, Andrea realized the mysterious faerie woman's true sympathies no longer mattered. She met Lenore's azure eyes with sad resignation

But then, Lenore slowly stood, tension building in the room.

"My lady chaired this proceeding under auspicious stars inclined towards fate and futures woven," she began, her fingers tracing glowing druid runes in the air. Andrea watched in awe as Lenore seemingly pulled timeline strands visible across the wavering votive candles. With a final fluid tug, the glowing threads entwined around Lenore's ringed hands. "The accused shall be spared destruction and granted mercy growth instead," Lenore announced, her voice ringing with otherworldly authority. "So foreseen, the best paths aligned."

Stunned silence fell as the implications sank in. Lenore had contradicted Celia's death sentence, rendering the final judgment vote evenly split – an impossible outcome in coven governance history.

"Impossible!" Vara shrieked. "This goes against all precedent!" Sister Celine looked both awed and frightened. "The stars themselves have spoken... who are we to argue?" All eyes pivoted to Sapphira, who stood rigid with apoplectic rage, the future of New Orleans' supernatural world hanging in the balance of her response. "This... this is an outrage," she said, her form beginning to shift and twist with her fury. "I will not stand for this mockery of our sacred laws!"

Andrea and Lenore exchanged a look, both knowing that the real battle was only just beginning.

Chapter 13 The Captains Confession

Still mentally reeling in grateful disbelief over Andrea's daunting court victory saving him from certain execution, the night breeze through Angelo's fourth story office window carries unexpected relief in its familiar briny kiss. Grueling as the last 48 hours personal tribulation proved however, his duty-bound conscience recoils reacting predictably at the sharp rap on his door frame from a junior beat cop poking her head in.

As Angelo studied the weathered face of his superior, subtle clues he'd overlooked for years suddenly aligned—the captain's unwavering composure at gruesome crime scenes, his uncanny ability to appear silently, and those penetrating eyes that seemed to hold centuries of weariness. Rhemann hadn't just stumbled upon the supernatural world; he'd been immersed in it long before Angelo joined the force.

"Detective Dubois sir, Captain wants you down in his office pronto. Like drop everything now urgent if you catch my drift..." Officer Alvarez bites her lip stud apologetically under his weary scowl but stands resolute delivering direct orders. With an irritable sigh, Angelo straightens his perpetually rumpled tie and smooths errant hair raked by agitated fingers too often since word of Sapphira's nefarious condemnation plot leaked through their shadowy grapevine. As he descends the narrow stairwell debating strategy facing Rhemann's interrogation over increasingly blatant breach of carefully constructed human pretenses in the NOPD, Angelo paused suddenly on the landing flooded in false dawn glow. Squaring his shoulders, he recalls their last cryptic exchange on the outskirts of that grisly ritualized murder scene. Rhemann had hinted at sharing immortal longevity and insight living beyond natural years himself. Was it possible his gruff superior operated under similar pretense through an officer's facade for subversive motives? Did they stand stronger united in secrets or only doomed duplicity risking fragile mortal institutions mission-critical to preserve from chaos?

Filled with wary purpose, Angelo steps into the modest office where Captain Rhemann waits staring intently.

Before he can utter official platitudes undoubtedly rehearsed against potential dismissal talks, the veteran officer tosses his gleaming badge down between them gravely. "We better talk truth off record, vampire. Because these haunted streets are on fire…and all our asses with 'em soon enough if we can't work quick to douse hellish loose ends first…"

Angelo eases tentatively into the well-worn leather chair opposite Rhemann's imposing oak desk where that jarringly symbolic gleaming badge rests between them glinting austere under the muted green banker's lamp. Resigning himself to this unprecedented supernatural disclosure summit, he observes Rhemann pouring out two fingers neat bourbon for each of them. Angelo notes the usual commander steel now softened ever slightly behind a weathered frontage he suddenly recognizes as twin to his own after endless facades worn for mortal structures long outliving individual men.

"Never stood much on false ceremony when hard truths need airin'…" Rhemann mutters gruffly before taking a bracing swig. Pensive moments tick by to Ray Charles crooning scratchy over an unseen radio. The captain steeples thick fingers, gazing beyond Angelo to some long-ago place and people. "Walked most my years thinking ole third-lifer artillery captain like me held last living eyes on horrors humanity never deserved witnessing." His rueful throaty chuckle holds little mirth. "Two decades adrift on these streets after the war, when civilization seemed but walking ghosts aside me, some back-alley savior found my hollow drunken husk instead. Gave new lease on justice trying to balance my soul I reckon. Though maybe damnation ultimately when my heart kept silent about wicked new bedfellows. Until you showed up..." Rhemann appraises Angelo like a foreign portent he must determine guiding star or dire storm herald. "Thought loneliness held only my burden stiffening this uniform. Now fate laughs revealing you lurked in my own blindspot whole time..."

Angelo smells the rising question and deflects gently. "Suppose we spent too long navigating by fear instead of faith trying read maps that never showed whole terrain. No more though if we shoulder this cross together, mon capitaine..."

Angelo weighs his words carefully before continuing further insight exchange with newly revealed kindred spirit Rhemann.

"I wager lives counted blessed or cursed riding fellow powder kegs these long decades, Monsieur Capitan. But your unique longevity gifts rare perspective serving New Orleans' thin blue line same as my investigator role maintaining order midst criminal chaos." He raises his glass, swishing the caramel liquid thoughtfully. "We needn't bare the gnashing gory details that set us each wandering condemned between death and damnation's twilight realms so long..." Angelo peers over his whiskey glass pointedly before taking a slow sip. "Suffice you clearly gleaned my, shall we say, extraordinary nocturnal citizenship origins by now. And I discern clues plenty pointing to a vampiric benefactor of some age and influence in your past as well..." He gives Rhemann meaningful look. "One perhaps directly tied to current spree threatening to expose far more than good detectives of the Homicide Division." Now Rhemann slowly sets his own emptied glass down on the desk blotter with audible thud. "You would happen to refer to those transients and destitute turning up exsanguinated in alleyways while NOPD wastes manpower hunting some satanic panic serial myth?" He snorts derisively. "Guess mask finally slipped when I got careless letting you catch a whiff though at that society gal dump-job."

Angelo remains silent, watching the captain closely circle his realm more agitated as truths lay bare. "Yeah, my fangs run deep as Mardi Gras beads in this town's bloody sin, Dubois. Almost two centuries taking secrets to the swampy grave on elite masters' behalf since one venom kiss enlisted me eternal..." He stops brusque, jaw tightening against something still left unsaid. Sensing shadows withheld still; Angelo gently presses. "And does our Lady Death herself know full well she counts no mere minion but fierce ace asset within the venerable force now? The elegant immortal with teeth and tastes sharper than her smoky mascara gaze?" He doesn't need preternatural senses to hear the creaking leather as Rhemann's fist tightens involuntary around his flask...

In the charged silence, Angelo scrutinizes his superior carefully as the usual aloof veteran facade crumbles slightly, exposing glimpses of a desperate soul bartered eternal defiance of mortality's judgment. A ruined leg in some nameless foreign battlefield. A lifetime consigned drifting hungry condemnation along Big Easy backchannels until mercy manifested seeking reciprocal fealty.

Rhemann grimaces bitterly, composure slipping enough his visitor now detects the slight Francais lilt coloring speech." Oui, she raised me from perdition into forever sergeant at arms over this territory on her whim. But I pledged the standard blood oaths willingly..." He pauses with dark revelation, lips thinning against confession never before uttered." Mostly. Barring once when old debts required...rebalancing from my ragged alley days." Another swallow from the flask now trembling ever so faintly. "Let us say in my folly, our cunning benefactress was forced to intercede resolving a shadowy indiscretion matter rather indelicate for a then rising law official..."

Realization dawns on Angelo. Rhemann was indebted toward his eternal patroness before and after this immortal rebirth sacrament. Likely at her sly orchestration. Which explained the myriad tasks discreetly completed furthering only Sapphira's veiled agenda over justice or duty all these years. The captain mutely confirms his conclusion, features etched granite as pressure builds awaiting judgment of his own from newly initiated secret fraternity member. Instead, Angelo leans forward earnestly, careful not to spook this vulnerable gruff confessor. "I deduce our clandestine queen secured a most advantageous double agent in the halls of justice none before recognized. So, tell me mon ami...where precisely do your true loyalties lie when her games portend spilling not just society blood headlines but all authority thin as our theater? And who might stand steadfast together when damnations come due?"

Rhemann nods slowly over interlaced fingers, exhaling heavily like a soul-deep burden already lightening ever slightly not carrying terrible truth and freedom's cost alone anymore behind the straining badge. "Perhaps destiny finally finished her jest uniting lone wolves in purpose protecting what scraps remain worth salvaging from endless depravity churning through. The rest...comes in time revealing when our pale mistress makes true endgame play, I wager." His usually stern eyes glint almost mischievous now with camaraderie as he stands offering his hand instead of customary curt dismissal. Angelo returns the gruff shake of brothers in arms crossed behind the veil. Stepping back into the bustling station proper, he breathes deep, skull buzzing processing shocking revelations from an unexpected powerful corner. Before equilibrium restores, Detective Clay's bright baritone cuts the din waving Angelo over excitedly.

"Hey, Dubois! Uniforms responding to a dockworker missing persons just rolled up on a body savagely beaten down by the wharf warehouses. Finally caught a break - no signs indicating transients like the usual floaters. This one looks more ritual style execution from the first glimpses..."

Angelo sighs, longing for respite disappearing. But duty still urgently calls protector and avenger both. He squeezes the eager junior detective's shoulder as the address texts through. "Well done, Clay. Have CSU en route while I check prelim scene. Text me location and we will crack this darkness come hell or high water, mon ami!" With purposeful strides belying bone-tired resignation within, Angelo heads off seeking the crime scene...and whatever fresh mortal mayhem awaits now. As Angelo departs the suddenly claustrophobic station house reeling internally between shocking disclosures and new murder summons, he pauses gulping the heavy humid night air. Grateful to a fault now for the dark's concealing veil shrouding immortal secrets and searing doubt behind slick squad car lights currently warping his strained features unnoticed as just another wayward shadow. There will be no bright sanctuary dawns unfurling insight on twisted fates looping ever tighter this cycle he knows...only deepening duty dredging the drowned remains mere mundane monsters leave bobbing amidst uncaring currents in their wake.

With renewed purpose quickening immortal feet unburdened by dread weight or resignation a heartbeat more, Angelo embraces the beckoning night anew. Determined still to challenge damnation itself on behalf of what faint flickers of justice or redemption might yet be coaxed from depths where only the damned dare dive. New Orleans sprawls before her defender once more. But this respite proves fleeting as flashing lights and keening sirens just ahead signal some fresh horror imposed under merciless stars...

Chapter 14: Echoes of Cruelty

Angelo is assaulted by a pervading sense of wrongness even blocks away from the new crime scene. The eerie sensation feels like ghostly hands brushing against his consciousness, flooding his instincts with urgent dismay about the violations ahead. His centuries of existence had attuned him to the particular psychic residue of violence—especially when supernatural elements were involved. This was different, somehow more personal, as if whoever had committed this atrocity had left a deliberate signature for him to find.

The Camaro's engine growled as Angelo accelerated through the quiet streets of the Garden District. Dawn was still hours away, but even at this hour, New Orleans never truly slept. A few jazz clubs still thumped with muted brass notes, while street cleaners washed away the evidence of another night of revelry. But the music and laughter felt distant, disconnected from the grim reality toward which Angelo was racing.

His phone buzzed again. Detective Washington, his voice uncharacteristically tense: "Dubois, where the hell are you? Captain's already here, and he's asking for you specifically."

"Five minutes out," Angelo replied tersely, ending the call as he swerved around a delivery truck.

As feared, multiple squad cars box in a dingy alley cordoned off from curious onlookers. Their flashing lights painted the brick buildings in alternating crimson and blue, a disorienting light show that set Angelo's teeth on edge. Officers moved with uncharacteristic solemnity, their usual professional detachment replaced by a palpable sense of distress.

The sight that greeted Angelo as he approached sent ice through his veins. Detective Clay stood solemnly beside a tragically small shrouded form - the unmistakable outline of a child victim. The copper-penny scent of blood hung in the air, mingled with something else—something Angelo had encountered too many times before. The distinctive perfume of Sapphira's magic, like jasmine laced with ozone.

"Jesus, Angelo," Clay muttered as he approached. "Kid can't be more than seven. Who does something like this?"

Angelo didn't answer immediately, his enhanced senses already cataloging details the human police officers would never notice. The air pressure around the body was slightly lower than the surrounding area—a telltale sign of magical energy having been drained. Small particles of a glittering substance that looked like ordinary dust to human eyes, but which Angelo recognized as the residue of a powerful binding spell dusted the ground.

"Any ID yet?" Angelo asked, keeping his voice professionally neutral despite the rage already building within him.

"Nothing concrete. No missing persons match in the system yet. But..." Clay hesitated, something clearly troubling him. "The responding officer thought he recognized the kid from a community center over in the Ninth Ward. Thomas Mitchell, I think. Social services case. Mother died last year, father's not in the picture."

The name struck Angelo like a physical blow. He'd visited that community center three weeks ago, following up on reports of unusual activity. He remembered the boy—quiet, watchful, with intelligent eyes that seemed to take in everything. Angelo had given him a candy bar and ruffled his hair.

Had Sapphira chosen this child specifically because of that brief connection? The thought made Angelo's cold blood run even colder.

Kneeling beside the small broken body, Angelo carefully examines the evidence, bile rising in his throat. The bruises and ligature marks tell a clear story of deliberate violence rather than accident. He notices faint elongated puncture wounds that bear the unmistakable signature of Sapphira's unique feeding style - wounds he's documented in too many confidential files over the decades.

But there was something different about these marks—they weren't positioned over major blood vessels as would be typical for a vampire feeding. Instead, they formed a pattern across the child's chest, a symbol that Angelo recognized with growing horror. It was an ancient vampiric glyph meaning "lesson" or "instruction."

This wasn't just murder. It was a message intended specifically for him.

"Detective Dubois?" A young officer approached hesitantly. "There's something you should see. We found it clutched in the victim's hand."

The officer held out an evidence bag containing a small object—a lapis lazuli stone identical to the one in Angelo's ring, except this one was cracked down the middle.

Angelo's hand instinctively moved to his own ring, the ancient talisman that allowed him to walk in daylight. The implication was clear: Sapphira was threatening not just his cover identity but his very existence.

Rage boiled suddenly within Angelo, causing the very breeze around him to still unnaturally. The ambient sounds of the city—distant traffic, the hum of electricity, even the breathing of the officers around him—seemed to fade into a muffled quiet. The air temperature dropped several degrees, frost crystallizing on the edges of nearby puddles.

The younger officers stepped back unconsciously, responding to primal instincts warning them of a predator in their midst. Only Clay, who had worked with Angelo for years, stayed close, though even he looked uneasy.

Whirling up from his crouch, Angelo unleashes a feral snarl into the shadows. His normally carefully maintained human façade slipped, revealing something ancient and terrible beneath.

"Show yourself, harbinger of darkness! Come face retribution for this innocent's suffering!"

Only silence answers his raw challenge until wisps of jasmine and bone-chilling static herald Sapphira's arrival. The air seemed to fold in on itself, reality briefly warping as she stepped through a tear in the fabric of space. She materializes mere inches from Angelo's coiled fury, smug defiance etching her flawless features as she surveys the covered corpse with almost tender interest, deliberately provoking his protective instincts.

The humans couldn't see her—another of her tricks, existing in a state slightly out of phase with normal reality. To Angelo's supernatural senses, however, she was terrifyingly present, her power radiating like heat from a furnace.

"My dear detective," Sapphira purrs, her voice carrying an echo of centuries of malice. "We simply reap what we sow. You reject the natural order I offer without consequence?" One blood-pearl fang glints as her smile widens. "Then witness the price of your misguided mercy!"

She traces one elegant, deadly finger along the edge of the shroud covering the child. "Such sweet innocence. His fear was... exquisite. Did you know he called for you at the end? 'Detective Angel,' he said. Quite touching, really. He thought you would save him."

Angelo's fists clenched so hard that his nails cut into his palms, drawing blood. "This ends now, Sapphira. This child had no part in our conflict."

"Oh, but he did," she counters, her eyes gleaming with cruel amusement. "The moment you showed him kindness; he became a piece on our chessboard. Just as every human you've ever protected becomes my potential target."

She savors the moment, drinking in Angelo's anguish with evident pleasure. "Continue leading your human puppets if you must. But each innocent life I claim will burn this lesson deeper into your soul, my obstinate protégé..." Her voice drops to a whisper that only Angelo can hear. "Defy me again, and next time it will be your witch I take. How long do you think Andrea would last under my... ministrations?"

With a final caress of the small dead face between them, she vanishes on icy winds, leaving Angelo staring brokenly at the child who appears peacefully asleep except for the stillness no living being could maintain.

For a moment, Angelo remained frozen, the full impact of her threat against Andrea threatening to overwhelm his control completely. His vision tinged red, vampire instincts screaming for bloodshed, vengeance, a violence to match the savagery of what had been done to this innocent child.

"Dubois? You, okay?" Clay's concerned voice barely penetrated the fog of rage. "You look like you're about to pass out or something."

With a monumental effort, Angelo forced himself back into his human persona. "I'm fine," he managed, though his voice sounded strange even to his own ears. "Just... this one's hitting me hard."

Clay nodded solemnly. "Yeah, me too. Listen, Forensics needs access. We should step back and let them work."

Angelo moved mechanically away from the body, his mind racing. He needed to warn Andrea immediately. Needed to establish protective measures. Needed to hunt down Sapphira before she could fulfill her threat.

As Sapphira vanishes, Angelo feels a warm presence behind him. The unique blend of floral scents mixed with the distinctive aroma of magical workings announced her arrival before he even turned around. Andrea stands there, her face a mask of determination and compassion.

"You're not alone in this," she says firmly, her voice pitched low enough that the human officers wouldn't overhear. "I felt the magical disturbance from across the district. She was here, wasn't she?"

Angelo nods, relief washing through him at her presence even as fear for her safety intensifies. "We need to talk. Somewhere private."

Andrea glances at the crime scene, understanding immediately. "The coffee shop on St. Charles is still open. Meet me there in fifteen minutes?"

"Make it ten," Angelo replies, already planning the fastest route. "And Andrea... be careful. Stay in public spaces. She made threats."

A flash of fear crosses Andrea's face, quickly replaced by resolve. "I can handle myself, Angelo. But I'll be careful. Ten minutes."

They separate, maintaining their professional distance for the benefit of the watching officers. Angelo completes his preliminary examination of the scene with mechanical efficiency, his mind already racing ahead to protective spells, safe houses, and contingency plans.

The coffee shop is nearly empty when Angelo arrives nine minutes later. Andrea has secured a corner table away from windows, two steaming mugs already waiting. The establishment caters to the night shift workers of New Orleans—nurses, dock workers, and, unofficially, the supernatural community. The barista, a young werewolf trying to pay her way through college, nods respectfully to Angelo as he passes.

"I ordered you the usual," Andrea says as he sits opposite her. "Black with a shot of B negative."

Despite everything, Angelo feels a small smile tug at his lips. Their standing joke about his dietary requirements feels comfortingly normal in the midst of chaos.

"She killed that child to send me a message," Angelo says without preamble, keeping his voice low. "And she threatened you directly."

Andrea's hands tighten around her mug, but her voice remains steady. "Tell me everything."

Angelo recounts the encounter in detail, including the symbolism of the puncture wounds and the broken lapis lazuli stone. As he speaks, Andrea's expression grows increasingly grim.

"This isn't just about territory anymore," she says when he finishes. "She's making it personal."

"It's always been personal with Sapphira," Angelo replies. "I just didn't realize how far she'd go."

"We need to accelerate our plans," Andrea says, leaning forward. "The binding spell I've been researching—I think it's almost ready. With the right components, we could trap her, strip her powers permanently."

"The risk—" Angelo begins.

"Is worth taking," Andrea interrupts firmly. "Children are dying, Angelo. More will die if we don't stop her. Whatever the risk to us, we have to try."

Angelo knows she's right, but the thought of Andrea facing Sapphira's wrath terrifies him more than his own destruction. "We do this together," he says finally. "No solo heroics from either of us. Promise me."

"Together," Andrea agrees, reaching across the table to take his hand.

The coffee shop door jingles as new customers enter, breaking the moment. Both turn instinctively to assess the potential threat, but it's just a group of exhausted hospital workers coming off shift.

"We should go," Angelo says reluctantly. "I need to get back to the scene, and you need to secure your shop. Sapphira won't wait long to make her next move."

As they stand to leave, Angelo hesitates, then pulls Andrea into a fierce embrace, heedless of who might see. "Be safe," he whispers against her hair.

"You too," she replies, her arms tightening around him briefly before they separate.

They part ways outside the coffee shop, Andrea heading toward her flower shop in the French Quarter, Angelo back to the crime scene. The city streets are beginning to stir with early morning activity, shopkeepers raising shutters, delivery trucks making their rounds. The normalcy feels surreal after the horrors of the night.

Back at the crime scene, the body has been removed, but the sense of wrongness lingers. Captain Rhemann approaches as Angelo arrives, his expression carefully neutral.

"Anything about this one strike you as... unusual, Dubois?" the captain asks, his emphasis on the last word carrying hidden meaning.

Angelo studies his superior carefully. He's long suspected that Rhemann knows more about the supernatural world than he lets on. "Several things," he answers cautiously. "Particularly the timing and location. Almost as if it was staged for an audience."

Rhemann nods, seemingly satisfied with the answer. "Keep me in the loop on this one. Directly. No intermediaries."

Before Angelo can respond, a commotion breaks out at the perimeter. A woman's voice, distraught and desperate: "Let me through! That's my nephew! Thomas! THOMAS!"

Angelo moves quickly, intercepting the woman before she can see the bloodstained ground where the child's body had lain. She's young, perhaps mid-twenties, with the same dark eyes as the boy. Her grief is raw, overwhelming.

"Ma'am, I'm Detective Dubois," Angelo says gently, guiding her away from the scene. "I'm so sorry for your loss. Is there somewhere we can talk?"

The next hour passes in a blur of procedural necessities—notification of next of kin, preliminary questioning, arranging for victim services to provide support. The woman, Lisa Mitchell, is the boy's maternal aunt. She had been fighting for custody since her sister's death.

"He was supposed to be with a friend from the center," she says through tears. "A sleepover. I got called into work—I'm a nurse—and couldn't pick him up until morning. When I went to get him, they said he never arrived."

Angelo takes her statement mechanically, part of his mind still processing Sapphira's threats, planning protective measures for Andrea, strategies for the coming confrontation. But another part—the part that has clung to his humanity through centuries of darkness—feels each of Lisa Mitchell's tears like a physical wound.

"I promise you," he tells her when the formal questioning is complete, "I will find who did this. They will face justice."

What he doesn't say is what form that justice will take. Some crimes go beyond human law, requiring a more permanent resolution.

As dawn approaches, Angelo finds Andrea standing alone at the scene's edge, having returned after securing her shop. Her face is turned toward the lightening sky, her expression contemplative. She's cast a subtle glamour around herself—nothing that would alert other supernaturals, but enough that the human officers pay her little attention.

"What keeps you going?" she asks softly when Angelo joins her. "How do you face such darkness day after day, century after century, without losing yourself to it?"

It's a question Angelo has asked himself countless times over his long existence. There were decades—particularly in the early years after his turning—when he had indeed lost himself, becoming the very monster, he now hunts.

"Hope," Angelo answers after a thoughtful pause. "Hope that we can make a difference. Hope that there's still good worth protecting." He looks at the crime scene, where officers are completing their work. "Every child saved is a victory. Every innocent protected matters."

As he speaks, he finds himself drawing closer to Andrea, pulled by an invisible force. She doesn't back away, her gaze locked with his. The rising sun gilds her features, making her seem almost luminous against the dreary backdrop of the crime scene.

"And now?" she asks, her voice barely above a whisper. "What gives you hope now?"

"You do," he replies simply.

Their lips meet in a gentle kiss that quickly deepens with the emotion and tension that has been building between them. When they finally part, both are slightly breathless, eyes bright with shared purpose and something more profound.

"Whatever happens," Andrea says, her voice steady despite the blush coloring her cheeks, "we face it together. Sapphira wants to isolate you, use your compassion against you. But she doesn't understand—connection doesn't weaken us. It makes us stronger."

Before they can speak further, Captain Rhemann approaches with new information about trace evidence found at the scene. As they turn to face their duties once more, Angelo feels Andrea's hand slip into his. Whatever horrors Sapphira might unleash, they would face them together.

The sun rises over New Orleans, painting the sky in hues of pink and gold. Angelo and Andrea Walk hand in hand back to the crime scene, ready to continue their fight - not just for justice, not just for the innocent victims, but for a future together, a light pushing back against the encroaching darkness.

And somewhere in the shadows, Sapphira watches, her ancient eyes narrowing at this display of defiance. The game has changed, the stakes raised. But she has played the long game for centuries. She can wait for the perfect moment to strike—and when she does, neither vampire nor witch will see it coming.

Chapter 15: Planning the Rebellion

The first rays of dawn were just beginning to streak across the sky as Angelo arrived at Andrea's cozy apartment in the heart of the French Quarter. Despite the early hour, his vampiric senses were on high alert, scanning for any signs of danger or unwanted surveillance. The streets were quiet, save for the occasional early-morning reveler stumbling home from a night of excess.

As he approached Andrea's door, Angelo caught the comforting scent of herbs and candle wax that always seemed to permeate her living space. Underneath it all, he detected Andrea's unique scent - a mix of jasmine and something uniquely her that never failed to stir his senses. He knocked softly, using their secret pattern – three quick taps followed by two slow ones.

The door opened almost immediately, revealing Andrea. Angelo's breath caught in his throat. She was wearing a silky robe that clung to her curves, her hair slightly tousled as if she'd just gotten out of bed. The sight of her like this, vulnerable and intimate, sent a jolt of electricity through him.

"Right on time," she said, her voice husky with sleep. She ushered him inside, and Angelo couldn't help but notice the way the robe shifted as she moved, revealing tantalizing glimpses of skin.

"I was just about to start the tea," Andrea continued, seemingly oblivious to the effect she was having on him. She led the way to the kitchen, and Angelo followed, his eyes tracing the graceful line of her neck, the curve of her hips.

In the kitchen, Andrea busied herself with preparing her special 'focus' tea. Angelo leaned against the counter, watching as she moved around the small space. The normalcy of the moment struck him, a stark contrast to the dangerous plans they were about to make. Andrea reached up to grab a jar from a high shelf, and her robe rode up, revealing a long expanse of leg. Angelo swallowed hard, forcing himself to look away.

"What?" Andrea asked, catching his gaze when she turned back.

"Nothing," he smiled, trying to keep his voice steady. "Just appreciating this... us."

Andrea's expression softened. She sat down the kettle and crossed to him, wrapping her arms around his waist. The heat of her body against his was almost overwhelming. "No matter what happens," she said softly, her breath warm against his neck, "this is what we're fighting for. Our future."

Angelo pulled her closer, breathing in her scent. He could feel every curve of her body pressed against him, and it took all his self-control not to kiss her right then and there. For a moment, they stood there in charged silence, the air between them crackling with unspoken desire.

The whistle of the kettle broke the spell. Andrea reluctantly pulled away, and Angelo immediately missed her warmth. As she finished preparing the tea, Angelo began setting up the living room for their strategy session, grateful for the distraction.

By the time Lenore arrived, looking as enigmatic and ageless as ever, Angelo and Andrea had transformed the cozy living room into a war room. Andrea had changed into more practical clothing, but Angelo couldn't help but remember how she looked in that robe, the image seared into his mind.

For the next several hours, the three of them pored over their plans.

Occasionally, Angelo would touch his lapis lazuli ring for reassurance, drawing comfort from the centuries of Dubois protection it represented as they plotted against Sapphira's tyranny.

As Angelo outlined the vampire factions, Andrea's mind was already racing ahead, connecting his information with her knowledge of witch covens. They shared a look, years of partnership allowing them to communicate volumes without a word. Their fingers brushed as they reached for the same map, and Angelo felt a spark of electricity at the contact.

Lenore watched their seamless interaction with a mix of admiration and concern. "You two work well together," she observed. "But remember, Sapphira will use any weakness against us. Your bond could be a strength... or a vulnerability."

Angelo and Andrea exchanged another glance, this one tinged with worry and something deeper, more intense. They both knew the risks, but neither was willing to step back from their commitment – to the cause, or to each other.

As the day wore on, they refined their plans, debated tactics, and prepared for every contingency they could imagine. The close quarters and high stakes only seemed to intensify the underlying tension between Angelo and Andrea. Every accidental touch, every shared look, felt charged with meaning.

Finally, as the sun began to set, Lenore rose to leave. "We've done all we can for now," she said, her voice heavy with the weight of their task. "Get some rest. We'll need all our strength in the days to come."

After seeing Lenore out, Angelo collapsed onto Andrea's couch, the events of the day catching up with him. Andrea curled up next to him, her body fitting perfectly against his side, her head on his shoulder. The closeness was both comforting and maddening.

"Are we crazy for doing this?" she whispered, her breath warm against his neck.

Angelo was quiet for a moment, acutely aware of every point where their bodies touched. "Probably," he admitted. "But I can't think of anyone I'd rather be crazy with."

Andrea chuckled, then grew serious. She shifted, turning to face him, her face mere inches from his. "Angelo... when this is over... what do you want?"

He turned to face her, cupping her cheek gently. His thumb traced her lower lip, and he felt her breath hitch. "You," he said, his voice low and intense. "Us. A future where we don't have to hide or fight constantly. Where we can just... be."

Andrea's eyes darkened with desire. "That sounds perfect," she murmured, leaning in.

Their lips met in a kiss that was anything but soft or tender. It was passionate, urgent, filled with all the tension and longing that had been building between them. Angelo's hands tangled in Andrea's hair as she pressed herself closer, eliminating any space between them.

When they finally pulled apart, both were breathing heavily. Angelo rested his forehead against Andrea's, their breath mingling in the quiet room.

"Whatever happens," he said softly, his voice rough with emotion, "know that I love you. That won't change, no matter what Sapphira or anyone else throws at us."

Andrea nodded, her fingers tracing patterns on his chest. "I love you too. We're in this together, till the end."

As night fell over New Orleans, Angelo and Andrea remained entwined on the couch, the plans and maps forgotten for the moment. Tomorrow, they would begin the dangerous work of rebellion. But for now, in this moment, they allowed themselves to simply be – two people in love, dreaming of a future they would fight with everything they had to make real.

The road ahead would be fraught with danger, but as long as they had each other, they knew they could face anything. The fate of New Orleans – and their future together – hung in the balance. But in that quiet moment, hope and desire burned bright, twin flames in the darkness that lay ahead.

Chapter 16: Charting a Course

The first rays of dawn were just beginning to peek over the horizon as Angelo and Andrea settled into her cozy living room. The events of the past few days had left them both physically and emotionally drained, but they knew there was no time to rest. With Sapphira's reign of terror temporarily halted, they now faced the daunting task of reshaping the supernatural world of New Orleans - and beyond.

Angelo couldn't help but marvel at how far they'd come. Just a few short months ago, he'd been a lone vampire detective, navigating the murky waters between the human and supernatural worlds. Now, he sat beside Andrea, a powerful witch who had become not just his ally, but the love of his unnaturally long life.

"We need to start planning our next move," Andrea said, her voice tinged with exhaustion but determination. She reached for an ancient tome, its leather cover worn smooth by centuries of use. "Sapphira may be gone for now, but the power vacuum she's left behind could be just as dangerous."

Angelo nodded, his brow furrowed in concentration. "You're right. And it's not just New Orleans we need to worry about. Sapphira's influence extended far beyond the city limits."

As if on cue, Andrea's phone buzzed with an incoming message. She glanced at it, her eyes widening slightly. "It's from Eliza, my contact in the Salem coven. News of Sapphira's defeat is already spreading through the global supernatural networks."

Angelo leaned in, intrigued. "What are they saying?"

Andrea quickly scanned the message. "It's a mixed bag. Some are celebrating, calling it the end of an era of tyranny. Others are... concerned. They fear the power balance has been irreparably disrupted."

"They're not wrong," Angelo mused. He stood up, pacing the room as he often did when deep in thought. "We've been so focused on New Orleans, we haven't fully considered the wider implications."

Andrea nodded, pulling out a large, ornate map from a hidden compartment in her bookshelf. As she spread it out on the coffee table, Angelo realized it was unlike any map he'd ever seen. Glowing lines crisscrossed the continents, connecting various points that pulsed with magical energy.

"This is the *Cartographia Arcana*," Andrea explained, noticing Angelo's fascination. "It shows the major supernatural hubs and ley lines across the world. See here?" She pointed to a brightly glowing spot on the map. "That's us. New Orleans has always been a nexus of supernatural energy. But look at how it connects to other places."

Angelo leaned in, tracing the lines with his finger. "Salem, New York, New Orleans... they form a triangle. And here, across the Atlantic - London, Paris, Prague. They're all connected."

"Exactly," Andrea said, her eyes shining with the thrill of sharing knowledge. "The supernatural world is far more interconnected than most realize. What happens in one hub can have ripple effects across the globe."

As they pored over the map, Angelo's detective instincts kicked in. He began to see patterns, connections he'd never noticed before. "These smaller points," he said, indicating a cluster of dimmer lights, "what are they?"

"Smaller covens, vampire nests, werewolf packs," Andrea explained. "They're not as powerful individually, but together, they form a network that helps maintain the balance of power."

Angelo sat back, running a hand through his hair. "So, when we took down Sapphira..."

"We didn't just change New Orleans," Andrea finished for him. "We potentially upset the balance of power across the entire supernatural world."

The weight of this realization settled over them both. What had seemed like a victory for their city now took on global proportions.

"We need to reach out to the other hubs," Angelo said decisively. "Explain what happened, why we did what we did. Maybe we can prevent any knee-jerk reactions."

Andrea was already pulling out her phone. "I'll contact the Salem coven. They're one of the oldest and most respected witch communities in the world. If we can get them on our side, others might follow."

As Andrea made her calls, Angelo found himself drawn back to the map. His eyes fell on a symbol he didn't recognize - a stylized eye within a triangle, located in Geneva, Switzerland.

"Andrea," he called out, "what's this symbol here?"

Andrea looked up from her phone, her expression turning serious. "That," she said, "is the headquarters of the International Council of Night."

"International Council of Night?" Angelo repeated, the name unfamiliar on his tongue.

Andrea nodded. "They're a sort of... governing body for the supernatural world. Think of them as the UN for creatures of the night. They keep tabs on major supernatural events worldwide, mediate disputes between factions, that sort of thing."

Angelo's eyes widened. "How have I never heard of them before?"

"They prefer to operate in the shadows," Andrea explained. "Most supernatural beings go their whole lives without ever dealing with the Council directly. But for something like this..." She trailed off, her implication clear.

"Let me guess," Angelo said with a wry smile, "they're going to want to have a word with us."

As if in answer to his statement, a shimmering portal opened in the middle of Andrea's living room. Out stepped a figure cloaked in shadows, its features indistinct save for a pair of glowing eyes.

"Andrea Deveraux, Angelo Dubois," the figure intoned, its voice seeming to come from everywhere and nowhere at once. "The

Council requests your immediate presence in Geneva. Recent events in New Orleans have... attracted our attention."

Angelo and Andrea exchanged a look. This was it - the moment their actions would be judged not just by their city, but by the entire supernatural world.

"We'll come," Angelo said, his voice steady despite the nervous energy thrumming through him. "But we stand by what we did. Sapphira's reign of terror had to end."

The figure nodded, a gesture that somehow conveyed both acknowledgment and warning. "Your actions will be evaluated. The balance must be maintained."

As the portal widened to accommodate them, Andrea reached out and squeezed Angelo's hand. "Together?" she whispered.

"Always," he replied, squeezing back.

With a deep breath, they stepped through the portal, leaving behind the familiar streets of New Orleans for the unknown chambers of the International Council of Night. Whatever judgment awaited them, they would face it as they had faced everything else - side by side, their love and determination a beacon in the face of uncertainty.

As the portal closed behind them, the *Cartographia Arcana* on Andrea's coffee table pulsed with energy. The glowing point that represented New Orleans flared brightly for a moment before settling into a new, steady rhythm. The supernatural world was changing, and Angelo and Andrea were at the heart of that change. Their journey was far from over; in fact, it was only just beginning.

Chapter 17: Shadows in the Florist Shop

The next day dawned with a sense of unease lingering in the air as Andrea prepared to open her florist shop. The morning sun cast a golden glow through the windows, but despite the warmth of its rays, Andrea could not shake the chill that crept through her veins. For she knew that today, she would once again come face to face with Sapphira, the dark force that threatened everything she held dear.

As Andrea arranged bouquets of vibrant flowers, their petals unfolding like delicate secrets, the tinkling of the shop's bell heralded the arrival of an unwelcome visitor. Andrea's heart sank as she turned to see Sapphira standing in the doorway, her presence casting a shadow over the bright colors and cheerful atmosphere of the shop. "Sapphira," Andrea greeted, her voice betraying none of the fear that churned within her. "What brings you to my humble establishment?" Sapphira's lips curved into a cold smile as she swept into the shop, her eyes gleaming with malice. "I think you know why I'm here, Andrea," she purred, her voice dripping with venom. "You've been meddling in affairs that do not concern you." Andrea met Sapphira's gaze unflinchingly, her hands steady as she continued her work. "I seek only to uphold the principles of our kind," she replied evenly. "To ensure that justice is served where it is due."

Sapphira's laughter rang out like the tolling of a funeral bell, sending shivers down Andrea's spine.

"Justice?" she scoffed. "You speak of justice while plotting to overthrow your own leader?"

Andrea's jaw clenched as she fought to maintain her composure. "I speak of the rules that govern us all," she retorted, her voice trembling with suppressed rage. "Rules that you have chosen to ignore in your pursuit of power."

Sapphira's eyes narrowed, her expression darkening with fury. "You dare to lecture me on rules?" she cried, her voice low and dangerous. "You, who would seek to undermine everything that I have worked so hard to achieve?"

Andrea stood her ground, her spine straight and her chin held high. "I seek only to protect our kind from your tyranny," she declared, her voice ringing with defiance. "To ensure that no innocent lives are sacrificed in your insatiable quest for power."

For a moment, the two women stood locked in a tense standoff, the air crackling with the intensity of their emotions.

But then, with a final glare of contempt, Sapphira turned on her heel and swept out of the shop, leaving Andrea alone with her thoughts and the lingering echo of their confrontation. As Andrea watched Sapphira disappear into the morning light, she knew that their battle was far from over. But with each passing moment, her resolve only grew stronger, fueled by the knowledge that she was fighting for something greater than herself—for the future of their kind and the preservation of all that they held dear.

As Andrea locked the shop door behind her, she knew Angelo would be facing his own battles at the precinct tonight. The war against Sapphira was being fought on multiple fronts, and neither of them could afford to falter.

Chapter 18: Shadows of the Night

Back at the police station, Angelo, the vampire detective, felt a familiar sense of unease settle over him as he poured over the details of the latest crime scene. The air was heavy with the stench of death, mingling with the sterile scent of cleaning agents—a stark reminder of the darkness that lurked just beyond the reach of human sight. With keen senses honed over centuries of existence, Angelo could feel the lingering presence of malevolence that hung like a shroud over the room. He knew in his bones that Sapphira was behind this heinous act, her thirst for power driving her to commit unspeakable atrocities against the innocent. As he meticulously collected evidence and cataloged the scene, Angelo's mind raced with thoughts of justice and retribution. He knew that he needed to gather irrefutable proof of Sapphira's guilt if they were to have any hope of eliminating her and ending her reign of terror finally. With each passing moment, the weight of their mission bore down upon him, driving him forward with a sense of purpose that burned like a flame within his soul. He could not allow another innocent life to be snuffed out by Sapphira's dark machinations—not while he still drew breath.

As Angelo sifted through the evidence, his vampire senses tingled with the faintest whisper of magic—a subtle thread woven into the fabric of the crime scene, hinting at the presence of something otherworldly at play.

With a sense of grim determination, he followed the trail of magic, trusting in his instincts to lead him to the truth. As he dug deeper into the shadows of the night, Angelo knew that he was walking a dangerous path—one fraught with peril and uncertainty. But with the memory of innocent lives lost spurring him onward, he pushed aside his fear and pressed forward, ready to confront the darkness that awaited him at every turn. For Angelo, the hunt was far from over. And as he ventured deeper into the heart of darkness, he vowed to do whatever it took to bring Sapphira to justice and ensure that no more innocent blood was spilled in her name.

Later that evening Andrea set down her wine glass and turned to Angelo. "Sapphira's actions have been reprehensible. But we cannot stoop to her level by seeking revenge."

Angelo nodded solemnly. "You're right, violence will only breed more violence. There must be an ethical way for justice and redemption to prevail."

Andrea's eyes lit up as she recalled an old covenant text. "The coven bans members who murder innocents. If we can prove Sapphira killed that poor child, the Elders would have to exile her!"

"Brilliant!" exclaimed Angelo. "With your magic and supernatural connections, and my investigative skills, we may be able to lawfully gather irrefutable evidence against her." He paced excitedly, ethical plans formulating.

As the last embers faded in the hearth, Andrea grasped Angelo's hand, hope renewed. "United by wisdom and compassion, we will expose her violations peacefully. Her cruelty ends, without compromising our values."

The path ahead remained difficult, but side by side, their integrity stood strong in defiance of darkness.

As Angelo continued his meticulous investigation, his determination burned brighter with each piece of evidence he uncovered. With Andrea's guidance and his own instincts as a detective, he pieced together a trail of clues that led straight to Sapphira's doorstep. With their evidence in hand, Angelo and Andrea presented their case to the Elders of the coven, laying bare Sapphira's crimes and calling for her exile according to the ancient laws that governed their kind.

The Elders, swayed by the irrefutable proof and the unwavering integrity of Angelo and Andrea's actions, agreed to convene a trial to decide Sapphira's fate.

In a solemn ceremony attended by members of the coven and representatives from the supernatural community, Sapphira stood trial for her crimes against humanity. The evidence presented by Angelo and Andrea was overwhelming, leaving no doubt as to Sapphira's guilt. In the end, the Elders gave their judgment—Sapphira was to be stripped of her title as head witch and banished from New Orleans, never to return under penalty of death. With a heavy heart but a sense of justice served, Sapphira departed into the night, leaving behind the darkness she had wrought.

As dawn broke over the city, Angelo and Andrea stood together, their mission accomplished and their bond stronger than ever. Though the road had been fraught with danger and uncertainty, they had emerged victorious, their integrity and compassion shining as beacons of hope in a world touched by darkness.

As they looked to the future, Angelo and Andrea knew that their work was far from over. But with their shared values guiding their path, they faced the challenges ahead with courage and determination, ready to confront whatever darkness may come with unwavering resolve. And in the end, it was their unity and their commitment to justice that prevailed, ensuring that the light would always triumph over the shadows.

Chapter 19: Confronting the Unstoppable

In the heart of the police station, amidst the hustle and bustle of officers and detectives going about their daily tasks, Angelo felt a sudden chill grip the air. The room seemed to freeze in suspended animation, every movement halted as if time itself had come to a standstill.

And then, with a rush of wind and a flicker of darkness, Sapphira materialized before Angelo, her presence casting a shadow over the room. Angelo's heart quickened with a mixture of fear and determination as he locked eyes with the one, they had sought to overthrow.

"Sapphira," Angelo greeted, his voice steady despite the adrenaline coursing through his veins. "You cannot stop what is already in motion. Your reign of darkness ends here."

Sapphira's laughter echoed through the frozen room, sending shivers down Angelo's spine. "Oh, my dear Angelo," she purred, her voice dripping with malice. "You underestimate the extent of my power." Angelo stepped forward; his gaze unwavering as he faced Sapphira head-on.

"Your tyranny will not go unchecked," he declared, his voice resonating with conviction. "I will not rest until justice is served and the innocent are protected from your cruelty." Sapphira's eyes gleamed with amusement as she regarded Angelo with a mixture of scorn and pity. "You truly believe you can defy me?" she taunted; her voice laced with disdain. "You, a mere mortal, think you can challenge the might of a witch as powerful as I?"

Angelo felt a surge of defiance rise within him as he met Sapphira's gaze. "I may not have your raw power," he admitted, his voice tinged with steel, "but I have something you lack—integrity, compassion, and the strength of my convictions."

Sapphira's expression darkened with rage as she realized the depth of Angelo's resolve. "You are a fool to think you can stand against me," she yelled, her voice echoing through the frozen room. "I will crush you before you even have a chance to try."

But despite Sapphira's threats, Angelo stood tall, his spirit unbroken and his determination unwavering. For he knew that even in the face of overwhelming odds, his belief in justice would see him through.

As time resumed its course, Angelo stood firm in the face of Sapphira's chilling presence. Though her power was formidable and her threats ominous, Angelo's resolve remained unshaken. With each passing moment, his determination burned brighter, fueled by the memory of innocent lives lost and the weight of responsibility resting on his shoulders.

"Sapphira," Angelo repeated, his voice steady and unwavering. "Your reign of terror ends now. I will not allow you to continue preying on the innocent." Sapphira's lips curved into a sinister smile as she regarded Angelo with cold amusement. "You speak boldly, Detective," she remarked, her voice dripping with malice. "But you underestimate the depths of my power. You cannot hope to challenge me and emerge unscathed."

Angelo squared his shoulders, his gaze locked with Sapphira's. "Perhaps not," he conceded, "but I will not stand idly by while you bring suffering to those who cannot defend themselves. I will do whatever it takes to stop you."

With a flick of her wrist, Sapphira conjured a swirl of dark energy, crackling with malevolent intent. "You are a mere mortal," she taunted, her voice echoing through the room. "Your efforts are futile. I am unstoppable."

But Angelo refused to back down, drawing upon every ounce of courage and determination within him. With a swift motion, he reached for the amulet hidden beneath his shirt—a talisman of protection passed down through generations of his vampire lineage. As Sapphira's dark energy surged forward, Angelo held the amulet aloft, its radiant light pushing back against the shadows that threatened to consume him. With a cry of defiance, he channeled his inner strength, pushing back against Sapphira's onslaught with all his might.

For a moment, the room crackled with a fierce struggle between light and darkness, a battle of wills that threatened to tear the very fabric of reality asunder. But in the end, it was Angelo's unwavering resolve that emerged victorious, his courage and determination overcoming Sapphira's dark power.

With a furious roar, Sapphira vanished into the ether, her defeat echoing through the room like a thunderclap. As the last echoes faded away, Angelo stood alone in the now-quiet police station, the weight of his victory settling upon him like a heavy cloak. But even as he caught his breath and surveyed the aftermath of their confrontation, Angelo knew that the battle was far from over. With Sapphira still at large and darkness still lurking in the shadows, he knew that he must remain vigilant, ready to face whatever challenges may come his way in his ongoing quest for justice and redemption. And with the memory of his victory burning bright within him, he knew that he would never waver in his commitment to protecting the innocent and standing against the forces of darkness.

As the echoes of Sapphira's departure faded away, the oppressive stillness that had enveloped the police station lifted, and time resumed its natural flow. With a rush of wind, the frozen scene burst back to life, and the officers and detectives resumed their duties as if nothing had happened, which to them, was correct. Amidst the flurry of activity, Angelo's gaze fell upon Captain Rhemann, who stood by the window of his office, his expression inscrutable. Angelo felt a pang of uncertainty as he approached, unsure of how much the captain knew about the supernatural forces at play within their midst.

"Captain," Angelo greeted cautiously, his voice tinged with apprehension. "Is everything all right?"

Captain Rhemann turned to face Angelo; his eyes gleaming with an otherworldly intensity that sent a shiver down Angelo's spine. "Everything is as it should be, Detective," he replied cryptically, his voice carrying a weight that belied his calm demeanor.

Angelo's instincts screamed at him to tread carefully, to choose his words with caution in the presence of one who wielded such power. "I see," he responded carefully, his mind racing with possibilities. But before Angelo could press further, Captain Rhemann's expression softened, a ghost of a smile playing at the corners of his lips. "You've done well, Detective," he acknowledged, his voice warm with approval. "Your courage and determination have not gone unnoticed."

Angelo's heart swelled with relief at the captain's words, grateful for the acknowledgment of his efforts. "Thank you, sir," he replied earnestly, his voice tinged with gratitude.

With a nod of dismissal, Captain Rhemann turned back to the window, his gaze fixed on the horizon beyond. As Angelo returned to his duties, a sense of uncertainty lingered in the air—a reminder of the mysteries that still awaited him in the shadows, and the challenges that lay ahead in his ongoing quest for justice and redemption. But with the captain's approval and the memory of his victory burning bright within him, Angelo knew that he would face whatever came his way with courage and determination, ready to confront the darkness that lurked just beyond the reach of human sight.

Later that day, as the sun cast long shadows over the streets of New Orleans, Andrea found herself in the comforting embrace of her florist shop, surrounded by the vibrant colors and delicate scents of nature's beauty. But amidst the tranquility of her sanctuary, her mind buzzed with thoughts of the daunting task that lay ahead.

Seated across from Andrea, in a cozy corner of the shop, was Lenore Beauregard, the second witch in charge and a respected member of the coven. Her presence lent an air of wisdom and authority to the conversation, though her expression betrayed a hint of skepticism as Andrea laid out her plans.

"Andrea, Cher," Lenore began, her voice rich with the distinctive cadence of old New Orleans, "I understand your concerns about Sapphira's actions, but convening the coven for a vote is no small matter. It could cause friction within the family."

Andrea nodded; her gaze steady as she met Lenore's eyes. "I know, Lenore," she replied earnestly, her voice tinged with determination. "But we cannot ignore the transgressions that Sapphira has committed against our kind. We must uphold the principles of our coven, even if it means facing difficult decisions."

Lenore sighed; her expression thoughtful as she considered Andrea's words. "You speak true, Cher," she conceded, her voice softened with understanding. "But we must tread carefully. Sapphira wields great power, and challenging her authority could have consequences that we cannot foresee."

Andrea's heart sank at Lenore's words, the weight of their predicament pressing down upon her shoulders. But even in the face of uncertainty, she refused to waver in her conviction.

"I know the risks, Lenore," she replied firmly, her voice steady with resolve. "But we cannot allow fear to dictate our actions. We must do what is right, no matter the cost."

As the conversation drew to a close, Andrea and Lenore exchanged a meaningful glance, a silent understanding passing between them. Though the road ahead would be fraught with challenges and obstacles, they knew that they would face them together, united in their commitment to uphold the values of their coven and protect those who could not protect themselves.

And so, with the sun sinking below the horizon and the promise of a new day on the horizon, Andrea and Lenore parted ways, each carrying with them the weight of their shared burden and the hope of a brighter future for their kind.

Chapter 20: The Gathering Storm

The ancient halls of the Versailles Mausoleum echoed with hushed whispers as supernatural beings from all corners of New Orleans filed in. The air was thick with tension and the scent of old magic. Angelo and Andrea stood at the entrance, their faces set with determination.

"Ready?" Angelo asked softly, his eyes searching Andrea's face.

She nodded, squeezing his hand. "As ready as I'll ever be. Let's end this, once and for all."

As they stepped into the dimly lit chamber, Angelo couldn't help but remember the first time he'd entered this sacred space. It was decades ago, when he was still a fledgling vampire, unsure of his place in this hidden world. Now, he returned as a leader, a protector of both the supernatural and human realms of New Orleans.

The circular room, with its tiered seating surrounding a central dais, was filled to capacity. At the highest point sat the Elders, their faces obscured by shadows. Angelo recognized Margareth, the eldest, her wrinkled face a map of centuries lived. Her eyes, sharp despite her apparent age, followed Angelo and Andrea as they made their way to their seats.

The room was a tapestry of supernatural diversity. Vampires with their pale skin and predatory grace sat alongside witches adorned with intricate magical tattoos. Werewolves, tense and alert even in human form, occupied an entire section. In the corners, creatures shimmered in and out of visibility, their presence adding an air of unpredictability to the proceedings.

As the last of the attendees settled in, a hush fell over the crowd. Margareth stood, her voice carrying the weight of centuries as she addressed the gathering.

"We stand at a crossroads," she began, her words echoing in the cavernous space. "For too long, we have allowed fear and division to rule us. Sapphira's reign of terror ends now."

A murmur of agreement rippled through the crowd, but Angelo noticed several faces twisted in skepticism or outright hostility. He leaned closer to Andrea, whispering, "Not everyone's on board. Keep an eye on the vampire delegation to the left."

Andrea nodded almost imperceptibly, her fingers brushing against a hidden pocket where Angelo knew she kept a potent protective charm. The weight of the moment pressed down on them both. This wasn't just about defeating Sapphira; it was about reshaping the very fabric of supernatural society in New Orleans.

As Margareth continued outlining the threat Sapphira posed, Angelo's mind wandered to the journey that had brought them to this point. He remembered the first time he'd encountered Sapphira, centuries ago. She had been charismatic, powerful, and utterly ruthless. He had admired her then, even as a part of him recoiled at her cruelty.

A sharp elbow from Andrea brought him back to the present. Lenore had taken the floor, her ageless face serious as she began to detail their plan of attack.

"Sapphira's power is deeply rooted in the city itself," Lenore explained, her hands weaving intricate patterns in the air as she spoke. Ghostly images appeared, showing a map of New Orleans overlaid with glowing ley lines. "We must sever her connection to these energy points if we hope to weaken her."

As Lenore spoke, Angelo scanned the room, noting reactions. Most seemed engaged, even eager, but there were pockets of resistance. A group of older vampires huddled together, their expressions dark. A few witches looked skeptical, whispering among themselves.

Suddenly, a voice rang out from the vampire delegation. "And why should we trust you?" The speaker, a tall vampire with aristocratic features, stood. Angelo recognized him as Emilian, one of Sapphira's former lieutenants. "For centuries, Sapphira has kept order. Without her, we risk exposure to the human world!"

Murmurs of agreement rippled through sections of the crowd. Angelo felt Andrea tense beside him, ready to defend their plan, but he placed a calming hand on her arm. This was a moment for diplomacy, not confrontation.

Angelo stood, his presence commanding attention. "Emilian, I understand your concerns. I once shared them. But ask yourself this: at what cost has Sapphira maintained this so-called order? How many innocents, supernatural and human alike, have suffered under her rule?"

He paused, letting his words sink in before continuing. "We're not proposing anarchy. We're offering a chance at true cooperation, a balance that benefits all of us."

Emilian's eyes narrowed, but he sat down, seemingly satisfied for the moment. Angelo knew this wasn't the end of the dissent, but it was a start.

As the meeting progressed, plans were laid out in meticulous detail. Maps of the city were spread across tables, key locations marked, and strategies debated. Witches huddled in corners, reinforcing protective wards and preparing potions that might give them an edge in the coming conflict. Vampires sharpened their fangs and claws, while werewolves discussed optimal formations for their pack.

In a quiet moment, Andrea pulled Angelo aside. "We need to talk about the Echo of Eternity," she whispered, her eyes darting around to ensure they weren't overheard.

Angelo nodded grimly. The Echo, an ancient artifact of immense power, had been a point of contention in their planning. Its ability to amplify magical energies could turn the tide of battle, but its use came with significant risk.

"Have you figured out how to control it?" he asked.

Andrea's expression was troubled. "Not entirely. The magic is... volatile. If we're not careful, it could backfire catastrophically."

Before Angelo could respond, Lenore approached them, her eyes filled with concern. "I couldn't help but overhear," she said softly.

"The Echo is not to be trifled with. Its power has driven many to madness."

"We may not have a choice," Angelo replied, his voice low. "Sapphira's too strong to take on without every advantage we can muster."

Lenore nodded solemnly. "Then we must prepare for all possibilities. Come, I have an idea."

As midnight approached, Angelo called for attention once more. The room fell silent, all eyes turning to him. He felt the weight of their expectations, their hopes, and their fears.

"Tomorrow, we make our stand," he declared, his voice ringing clear through the chamber. "Some of us may not survive what's to come. But know this – your courage tonight will be remembered for centuries. We fight not just for ourselves, but for the future of our kind."

A solemn silence fell over the room, broken only by the sound of a distant thunderclap. The storm was approaching, both literally and figuratively.

As the meeting drew to a close, Angelo pulled Andrea aside. "Meet me at sunset?" he whispered. "There's something I want to show you."

Andrea nodded, curiosity piqued. "I'll be there."

The next evening, as the sun began to set, casting long shadows across the city, Andrea made her way to the agreed meeting spot – a small, secluded garden tucked away in the heart of the French Quarter. She found Angelo waiting, a picnic basket at his feet and a nervous smile on his face.

"A picnic?" Andrea asked, raising an eyebrow. "In the middle of all this chaos?"

Angelo shrugged, his smile widening. "I figured we could use a moment of peace. Besides, when was the last time you ate something that wasn't magical energy bars or coffee?"

Andrea laughed, the sound lighter than it had been in days. "Fair point. What's on the menu?"

As they settled onto the blanket, Angelo began unpacking an array of local delicacies – beignets, gumbo, and even a bottle of aged bourbon. They ate in comfortable silence for a while, savoring both the food and the rare moment of tranquility.

Finally, Angelo spoke. "I've been thinking about the future. Our future."

Andrea set down her glass, her heart quickening. "Oh? And what thoughts have you had, Detective?"

Angelo took a deep breath. "I know it's crazy, with everything that's happened and all the challenges ahead. But I can't imagine facing any of it without you by my side." He reached into his pocket, pulling out a small velvet box. "Andrea, will you marry me?"

Andrea's eyes widened, a mix of emotions playing across her face. "Angelo, I... are you sure? Our worlds are so different, and with everything going on..."

"I've never been more sure of anything," Angelo replied, his voice steady. "We've faced the worst together and come out stronger. Whatever comes next, I want to face it with you as my wife."

Tears welled up in Andrea's eyes as she nodded, a radiant smile spreading across her face. "Yes," she whispered. "A thousand times, yes."

As Angelo slipped the ring onto her finger – a beautiful antique piece with a moonstone at its center – their eyes met. The air between them seemed to crackle with energy, both magical and emotional. Slowly, inexorably, they leaned towards each other.

Their lips met in a soft, tender kiss. Though brief, it was filled with all the passion, love, and shared experiences that had brought them to this moment. The garden around them seemed to come alive in response, flowers blooming out of season, their perfume filling the air, while soft lights danced among the leaves.

As they parted, both slightly breathless, Andrea laughed softly. "I think the local spirits approve."

Angelo grinned, his eyes shining with love and hope. "Well, they have good taste."

Their moment of joy was interrupted by the sound of Andrea's phone buzzing insistently. With a sigh, she checked the message. "It's Lenore. The council is assembled and waiting for us."

Angelo stood, offering his hand to help Andrea up. "Duty calls. Ready to shape the future of supernatural New Orleans, future Mrs. Dubois?"

Andrea took his hand, intertwining their fingers. "Lead the way, future Mr. Andrea," she teased back.

As they made their way to the council meeting, the weight of their responsibilities settled back onto their shoulders. But now, with the promise of a shared future glimmering before them, that weight seemed a little easier to bear.

The sun had fully set by the time they reached the meeting place – a neutral ground chosen for its magical protections. Representatives from all supernatural factions were gathered, tension thick in the air. Angelo squeezed Andrea's hand one last time before they entered. "Together?" he asked.

Andrea nodded, her chin held high. "Together."

And with that, they stepped into the room, ready to face whatever challenges the new era might bring – as partners, as leaders, and as the beating heart of a supernatural community on the brink of monumental change.

As they entered, all eyes turned to them. The room was a microcosm of the supernatural world – vampires with their pale, ageless beauty; witches adorned with mystical symbols; werewolves barely containing their restless energy; and fae creatures shimmering at the edges of perception.

Lenore stood at the center, her ageless face grave. "We've received word," she announced without preamble. "Sapphira is on the move. She's gathered her forces at the old St. Louis Cemetery No. 1."

A ripple of unease passed through the gathering. The cemetery was a place of power, where the veil between worlds was thin. If

Sapphira was there, it could only mean she was planning something catastrophic.

"Then that's where we make our stand," Angelo declared, his voice steady and resolute. He turned to address the room at large. "We've prepared for this. We know the risks, but we also know what's at stake. This isn't just about New Orleans – it's about the future of our world, supernatural and human alike."

As Angelo spoke, Andrea felt a swell of pride and love. This was the man she had chosen, the leader who could unite their fractured community. She stepped forward, her voice joining his.

"We have the Echo of Eternity," she reminded them, holding up the artifact. Its surface shimmered with barely contained power. "With it, we can match Sapphira's strength. But more importantly, we have each other. Our unity is our greatest weapon."

The room erupted in a chorus of agreement. Plans were quickly finalized, roles assigned, and last-minute preparations made. As the various factions readied themselves for battle, Angelo and Andrea found a quiet moment alone.

"Whatever happens," Angelo said softly, cupping Andrea's face in his hands, "know that I love you. That won't change, no matter what we face out there."

Andrea leaned into his touch, her eyes shining with unshed tears. "I love you too. We're in this together, till the end."

With a final, fierce kiss, they turned to face their destiny. The battle for New Orleans – and perhaps the entire supernatural world – was about to begin. But as they stood side by side, fingers intertwined, they knew that whatever came, they would face it as one.

The gathering storm had finally broken, and in its wake, a new era would dawn – one shaped by the love of a vampire and a witch who dared to dream of a better world.

Chapter 21: The Trial of Sapphira

The ancient halls of the Versailles Mausoleum echoed with hushed whispers as supernatural beings from all corners of New Orleans filed in. The air was thick with tension and the scent of old magic. Angelo and Andrea stood at the entrance; their faces set with determination.

"Ready?" Angelo asked softly, his eyes searching Andrea's face.

She nodded, squeezing his hand. "As ready as I'll ever be. Let's end this, once and for all."

They stepped into the dimly lit chamber, a circular room with tiered seating surrounding a central dais. At the highest point sat the Elders, their faces obscured by shadows. Angelo recognized Margareth, the eldest, her wrinkled face a map of centuries lived.

As they took their seats, Angelo felt a chill run down his spine. He glanced around, noticing several of Sapphira's known allies scattered throughout the crowd. Their eyes gleamed with barely concealed hostility.

"They're here in force," he whispered to Andrea. "Be on your guard."

She nodded almost imperceptibly, her fingers brushing against a hidden pocket where Angelo knew she kept a potent protective charm.

As the last of the attendees settled in, a hush fell over the crowd. Suddenly, the temperature in the room plummeted. Frost crept across the stone floor, and several candles flickered out. A gust of wind extinguished half the remaining lights in the room, and Sapphira materialized on the central platform.

She stood tall and proud; her ageless beauty marred only by the cold cruelty in her eyes. "What is the meaning of this farce?" she demanded, her voice echoing off the stone walls.

Margareth stood, her voice carrying the weight of centuries. "Sapphira LeCroix, you stand accused of grave crimes against our kind and the innocent humans under our protection."

Sapphira's laughter, sharp and mirthless, cut through the air. "Accused? By whom? These pitiful creatures who cower in the shadows?"

"By me," Angelo said, stepping forward. His voice was steady as he addressed the council. "I have gathered evidence of Sapphira's crimes. Murders of innocent children, violations of our most sacred laws, and actions that threaten to expose our entire society to the human world."

Sapphira's eyes narrowed. "You dare, Angelo? After all I've done for you?"

"You've done nothing but spread fear and pain," Angelo retorted. "It ends now."

Andrea joined him, her voice clear and strong. "We have witnesses, physical evidence, and magical proof of her transgressions."

"Proceed," Margareth nodded, settling back into her seat.

As Angelo and Andrea began presenting their case, the atmosphere in the room grew increasingly tense. Sapphira's supporters shifted restlessly, muttering among themselves. One particularly bold vampire stood up, pointing an accusing finger at Angelo.

"This is nothing but a witch hunt!" he shouted. "Sapphira has kept us safe for centuries!"

Murmurs of agreement rippled through parts of the crowd. Angelo felt Andrea stiffen beside him, ready for a fight. But before things could escalate, Lenore's calm voice cut through the chaos.

"Let them speak," she said, her tone brooking no argument. "We are here to seek the truth, not to shout each other down."

Reluctantly, the vampire sat, but the undercurrent of tension remained.

For the next several hours, Angelo and Andrea presented their case. They called forth witnesses, each testimony more damning than the last. A young vampire, trembling with fear, spoke of being forced to lure children for Sapphira's dark rituals.

"I... I had no choice," he stammered. "She threatened to destroy my entire bloodline if I refused."

Sapphira scoffed. "Weakness. I merely culled the herd, ensuring our kind's survival."

An elderly witch hobbled forward, her eyes blazing with long-held anger. "My granddaughter," she said, pointing a gnarled finger at Sapphira. "You took her, twisted her mind with your foul magic. When she finally broke free, she couldn't live with what you'd made her do. She took her own life!"

Murmurs of outrage rippled through the crowd. Sapphira remained unmoved. "Collateral damage. The weak perish so the strong may thrive."

As the testimonies continued, the air in the chamber grew thick with magical energy. Angelo noticed small objects beginning to levitate, reacting to the heightened emotions in the room. He caught Andrea's eye, silently urging her to be ready for anything.

Even a few brave humans were called to testify. A middle-aged man, his hands shaking, recounted a night of terror. "I saw her... change. Into something... not human. She killed my friends, drained them dry. I only survived because... because she said she wanted me to live with the fear."

As the evidence mounted, Sapphira's composure began to crack. Her eyes darted around the room, seeking out supporters, but finding only accusing stares. The magical energy in the room intensified, causing the walls to groan and the floor to tremble slightly.

"This is absurd!" she finally exploded, dark energy crackling around her. "I have protected this city for centuries! Without me, you would all be nothing!"

Lenore stood up then, her quiet voice carrying clearly across the chamber. "Protection through fear is not protection at all, Sapphira. It's tyranny."

"You ungrateful wretches," Sapphira cfied. "I've given you power beyond your wildest dreams!"

"Power at the cost of our souls," Andrea retorted. "We reject your 'gifts,' Sapphira. We choose a different path."

The room erupted into heated debate. Voices rose and fell, some defending Sapphira, others condemning her. Through it all, Angelo and Andrea stood firm, their united front a beacon of hope for those who sought change.

Suddenly, a blinding flash of light filled the chamber. When it faded, everyone saw that the central dais had split down the middle, a yawning chasm separating Sapphira from her accusers.

"Enough!" Margareth's voice boomed, magically amplified to cut through the chaos. "We have heard the evidence. It is time for judgment."

As the Elders conferred in hushed whispers, the tension in the room reached a fever pitch. Angelo could feel the magic in the air, thick and oppressive, making it hard to breathe. He noticed several of Sapphira's supporters edging closer, hands hidden in the folds of their robes.

"Andrea," he whispered urgently. "Be ready. I think they're going to try something."

She nodded grimly, her own hands moving in subtle gestures as she prepared defensive spells.

Finally, Margareth stood once more. "Sapphira LeCroix," she began, her voice heavy with the weight of judgment, "we find the evidence against you to be overwhelming and irrefutable. Your actions have brought shame upon our kind and endangered us all."

A collective gasp went through the room. Sapphira's face contorted with rage.

"By the power vested in this council," Margareth continued, "we hereby strip you of your titles and powers. You are to be exiled from New Orleans, never to return under pain of death."

For a moment, stunned silence reigned. Then, Sapphira's laughter, cold and terrible, filled the chamber. "You think you can judge me?" she shrieked, her form beginning to shift and twist. "I am eternal! I am power incarnate! You are nothing but dust beneath my feet!"

As Sapphira's body began to transform, her supporters sprang into action. Spells flew across the room, shattering the protective wards and plunging the chamber into chaos. Angelo tackled Andrea to the ground as a bolt of dark energy sizzled overhead.

"This is it," he shouted over the din. "Are you with me?"

Andrea's eyes met his, fierce determination shining in them. "Always," she replied. "Let's finish this."

As they stood to face Sapphira's unleashed fury, the fate of New Orleans – and perhaps the entire supernatural world – hung in the balance. The trial was over, but the real battle was just beginning.

Chapter 22: The Maelstrom of Magic and Will

The Versailles Mausoleum shuddered violently, ancient stones screaming under the onslaught of Sapphira's unleashed power. The air itself seemed to bleed, crackling with malevolent energy that tasted of ozone, sulfur, and primordial fear. Shards of shattered stained glass rained down in a kaleidoscope of deadly colors, slicing through flesh and stone alike. Sapphira's transformation was a horror beyond imagining. Her flesh bubbled and shifted like molten wax, unable to contain the dark forces within. Obsidian scales erupted across her skin in waves, while her eyes blazed with infernal fire, leaving scorching afterimages in the vision of all who dared look upon her. Wings, leathery and vast, unfurled from her back with a sickening crack of bone and sinew, scraping against the chamber walls and sending chunks of masonry crashing to the floor.

"You DARE to judge ME?" her voice boomed, a cacophony of a thousand screaming souls.

The very air rippled with each word, and those nearest to her clutched their ears in agony, blood seeping between their fingers. "I AM JUDGMENT! I AM THE ALPHA AND THE OMEGA OF YOUR PITIFUL EXISTENCE!"

With a gesture that seemed to tear through reality itself, tendrils of writhing shadow lashed out, wrapping around the nearest Elder. The old witch's scream was a sound of pure anguish, cut horrifyingly short as she crumbled to ash, her life force visibly absorbed into Sapphira's swelling form. Panic erupted in a frenzy of supernatural proportions. Vampires blurred into action, their supernatural speed leaving trails of afterimages in the chaos. Yet even they seemed to move in slow motion compared to Sapphira's lightning-fast attacks. Witches frantically chanted protection spells, their words creating shimmering barriers that shattered like glass against Sapphira's onslaught.

Werewolves, caught in the throes of involuntary transformation brought on by sheer terror, howled in agony as bones snapped and reformed. Their half-formed bodies made them easy targets, and Sapphira's laughter rang out with each fall. In the eye of this storm, Angelo grabbed Andrea's hand, his grip desperate. "We need to contain her!" he shouted, his voice barely audible over the din of destruction and despair.

"If she breaks free of the mausoleum—" Andrea nodded grimly, blood trickling from a cut above her eye. "The city wouldn't survive the night. The world might not survive her reign." Together, they pushed through the fleeing crowd, moving against the tide of terror. Angelo's vampiric strength cleared a path, his enhanced muscles straining as he shoved aside friend and foe alike. Andrea's magic crackled around them in a protective dome, deflecting debris and errant spells that filled the air like deadly fireworks.

Sapphira's laughter, a sound that seemed to come from the very pits of hell, echoed through the chamber. "Come then, my little rebels!" she taunted, her voice dripping with malice and mad glee. "Come and face your doom! Let me taste your despair!"

As they approached, reality itself seemed to warp and twist. The air grew thick and viscous, like wading through molasses made of nightmares. Light bent unnaturally around Sapphira, creating a disorienting kaleidoscope effect that threatened to overwhelm the senses.

Andrea began to chant, her voice wavering at first but growing stronger with each syllable. Glowing sigils appeared in the air around them, pulsing with an otherworldly light that seemed to push back against the encroaching darkness. Angelo felt a familiar surge of energy as his own innate vampiric abilities amplified in response to her spell, his senses sharpening to a painful degree.

Sapphira's attention snapped to them, her lips curling into a snarl that revealed rows of needle-sharp teeth. "Ah, the lovebirds," she crooned, her voice a discordant melody. "How touching. How utterly futile." With a speed that defied comprehension, she lashed out. A whip of pure darkness, edged with what looked like screaming faces, sliced through the air towards them. The very fabric of space seemed to tear in its wake. Angelo moved on pure instinct, centuries of honed reflexes kicking in as he tackled Andrea to the ground. The dark energy crackled overhead, missing them by mere inches. Where it struck the wall behind them, the stone didn't just scorch – it ceased to exist, leaving a void that hurt the eyes to look upon. As Sapphira's dark energy lashed out, a figure blurred in front of Angelo, taking the hit. It was Rhemann, his chest smoking from the impact. "Go!" he growled through gritted teeth. "End this!" Angelo hesitated, but Rhemann pushed him forward. "I've made my choice, Dubois. Now make yours count!"

"Now, Andrea!" Angelo yelled, rolling to his feet and pulling her up in one fluid motion. Andrea thrust her hands forward, channeling every ounce of her power into a single, desperate attack. A torrent of pure, white light erupted from her palms, so bright it turned night into day for a blinding instant. It struck Sapphira full in the chest, the impact sending out a shockwave that knocked everyone off their feet. For a moment, hope surged—Sapphira staggered back, her monstrous form seeming to waver and shrink. But then, to their horror, she laughed. The sound started low, building to a crescendo that shook the very foundations of the mausoleum.

"Is that all?" she mocked, her body seeming to absorb the light, growing larger and more terrifying with each passing second. "Let me show you true power, you insignificant motes of dust!"

The air imploded around them, an invisible force threatening to crush them out of existence.

Angelo felt his bones creaking, his enhanced physique straining against the pressure. Beside him, Andrea gasped, blood trickling from her nose and ears as she fought to support her protective spell.

All around them, others were not so fortunate. Bodies crumpled like paper dolls, the sickening sound of breaking bones and tearing flesh filling the air. The screams of the dying merged into a hellish chorus that threatened to drive them mad. Just when it seemed they would be crushed into oblivion, a new voice rang out, cutting through the chaos like a blade of pure will. "ENOUGH, SAPPHIRA!"

Lenore stepped forward, her slight frame belying the power that radiated from her in palpable waves. With a gesture that seemed to rewrite the laws of physics, she shattered the crushing force field.

"You would stand against me too, old friend?" Sapphira's voice dripped with venom, a hint of her former elegance bleeding through the monstrous visage.

"I stand for balance," Lenore replied, her calm voice a stark contrast to the madness surrounding them. "Something you've long forgotten in your lust for power."

What followed was a duel of cosmic proportions, a battle that would be spoken of in hushed whispers for centuries to come. Lenore and Sapphira traded blows of pure magical energy, each strike lighting up the chamber like the birth and death of stars. Reality itself seemed to buckle under the strain of their combat, spaces opening to other dimensions and closing just as quickly. Angelo and Andrea weren't idle spectators to this clash of titans. As Lenore kept Sapphira occupied, they worked in perfect synchronization, their minds linked by desperation and shared purpose. They wove spells of binding and banishment, their combined power creating a web of magic that began to close around Sapphira like a net.

Other survivors, inspired by their bravery, joined the effort. Vampires lent their blood and vitality to fuel the spells. Witches chanted in languages long forgotten by the waking world. Even the wounded contributed, offering what little strength they had left to the cause.

Sapphira, for all her immense power, found herself slowly but surely being cornered. Her attacks grew wilder, more desperate, lashing out in all directions. "I will not be defeated!" she shrieked, her form swelling to grotesque proportions, threatening to burst the very seams of reality. "I am eternal! I am—" Her words were cut short as Lenore, battered and bleeding but unbowed, struck with a spell of such potency that the very air ignited. "You are done," Lenore said simply, her voice carrying the weight of final judgment.

The combined magic of all present surged forward, a tidal wave of power that engulfed Sapphira in a maelstrom of light and shadow. Her scream of defiance turned to one of fear, then faded entirely as her form began to disintegrate.

In a final, cataclysmic burst of energy that threatened to tear the veil between worlds, Sapphira vanished. The sudden silence that followed was as deafening as the chaos that had preceded it.

As the dust settled and the magical energies dissipated, Angelo helped Andrea to her feet. They surveyed the devastation around them, the cost of their victory written in blood, rubble, and the haunted eyes of the survivors. "Is it... is it truly over?" someone whispered in the eerie quiet, fear making their voice tremble.

Lenore, looking centuries older than she had at the start of the night, nodded wearily. "She is banished," she confirmed, her voice hoarse. "Stripped of her power and cast into the void between worlds. But at what cost?"

A ragged cheer went up from the survivors, a sound of relief tinged with disbelief and lingering terror. But Angelo and Andrea exchanged a somber look, the weight of their pyrrhic victory settling heavily upon them. They had won, yes, but the price had been catastrophic.

As the adrenaline of battle faded, new questions loomed large in their minds: What would become of their world now, in the power vacuum left by Sapphira's fall? How would they rebuild from this devastation? And perhaps most chillingly – was Sapphira truly gone, or had they merely postponed an even greater reckoning?

As the first rays of dawn broke over a changed New Orleans, painting the sky in hues of blood and gold, Angelo and Andrea knew that their greatest challenges – and darkest trials – might still lie ahead.

The battle was over, but the war for the soul of their world had only just begun

Chapter 23: The Dawn of a New Era

As the sun climbed higher in the sky, casting a golden glow over the battered landscape of New Orleans, Angelo and Andrea made their way through the debris-strewn streets. The silence was eerie, broken only by the distant sound of sirens and the occasional crunch of glass beneath their feet. They passed by one of the city's famous above-ground cemeteries, its white stone tombs gleaming in the morning light. The air was unnaturally still, the usual bustle of the city replaced by an expectant hush, as if New Orleans itself was holding its breath in the aftermath of the supernatural battle.

"I never thought I'd say this," Angelo muttered, "but I miss the usual morning traffic."

Andrea managed a weak smile. "Careful what you wish for. Once the shock wears off, we'll have a lot of explaining to do." They rounded a corner to find Lenore coordinating a group of witches who were using their magic to clear rubble and repair damaged buildings. The elderly witch looked up as they approached, her face etched with exhaustion but her eyes bright with determination.

"Ah, our heroes arrive," Lenore said, her voice a mixture of warmth and weariness. "How are you both holding up?"

"We're still standing," Andrea replied, glancing at Angelo. "Which is more than I can say for half the city."

Lenore nodded solemnly. "The physical damage we can repair. It's the wounds to our community that worry me most."

Angelo's brow furrowed. "What's the situation with the other factions?"

Lenore sighed heavily. "Chaos, as you might expect. The vampires are divided – some see Sapphira's fall as an opportunity to seize power, others are calling for isolation. The werewolves are on edge, fearing retaliation for past grievances. And don't even get me started on the fae..." "We need to call a meeting," Andrea said firmly. "All factions, as soon as possible. We can't afford infighting, not when we're this vulnerable." Angelo nodded in agreement. "I'll reach out to the vampire elders. Andrea, can you contact the witch covens?"

"Consider it done," Andrea replied. "Lenore, can you act as a neutral mediator? Your wisdom and experience could be crucial in keeping tempers in check."

Lenore's eyes twinkled with a hint of her old mischief. "My dear, I've been keeping hot-headed supernatural's from tearing each other apart since before your grandparents were born. I'd be delighted to assist."

As they parted ways to begin their preparations, Angelo caught Andrea's arm. "Meet me at sunset? There's something I want to show you."

Andrea nodded; curiosity piqued. "I'll be there."

The day passed in a whirlwind of activity. Angelo spent hours on the phone, navigating the complex politics of vampire society. More than once, he had to resist the urge to bare his fangs at particularly obstinate elders. Andrea fared little better, mediating disputes between rival witch covens and trying to quell fears of another Sapphira-like tyrant rising to power.

As the sun began to set, casting long shadows across the city, Andrea made her way to the agreed meeting spot – a small, secluded garden tucked away in the heart of the French Quarter. She found Angelo waiting, a picnic basket at his feet and a nervous smile on his face.

"A picnic?" Andrea asked, raising an eyebrow. "In the middle of all this chaos?"

Angelo shrugged, his smile widening. "I figured we could use a moment of peace. Besides, when was the last time you ate something that wasn't magical energy bars or coffee?"

Andrea laughed; the sound lighter than it had been in days. "Fair point. What's on the menu?"

As they settled onto the blanket, Angelo began unpacking an array of local delicacies – beignets, gumbo, and even a bottle of aged bourbon. They ate in comfortable silence for a while, savoring both the food and the rare moment of tranquility.

Finally, Angelo spoke. "I've been thinking about the future. Our future."

Andrea set down her glass, her heart quickening. "Oh? And what thoughts have you had, Detective?"

Angelo took a deep breath. "I know it's crazy, with everything that's happened and all the challenges ahead. But I can't imagine facing any of it without you by my side." He reached into his pocket, pulling out a small velvet box. "Andrea, will you marry me?"

Andrea's eyes widened, a mix of emotions playing across her face. "Angelo, I... are you sure? Our worlds are so different, and with everything going on..."

"I've never been surer of anything," Angelo replied, his voice steady. "We've faced the worst together and come out stronger. Whatever comes next, I want to face it with you as my wife."

Tears welled up in Andrea's eyes as she nodded, a radiant smile spreading across her face. "Yes," she whispered. "A thousand times, yes."

As Angelo slipped the ring onto her finger – a beautiful antique piece with a moonstone at its center – the garden around them seemed to come alive. Flowers bloomed out of season, their perfume filling the air, while soft lights danced among the leaves.

"I think the local spirits approve," Andrea laughed, wiping away happy tears. Their moment of joy was interrupted by the sound of Andrea's phone buzzing insistently. With a sigh, she checked the message. "It's Lenore. The council is assembled and waiting for us."

Angelo stood, offering his hand to help Andrea up. "Duty calls. Ready to shape the future of supernatural New Orleans, future Mrs. Dubois?"

Andrea took his hand, intertwining their fingers. "Lead the way, future Mr. Andrea," she teased back.

As they made their way to the council meeting, the weight of their responsibilities settled back onto their shoulders. But now, with the promise of a shared future glimmering before them, that weight seemed a little easier to bear.

The sun had fully set by the time they reached the meeting place – a neutral ground chosen for its magical protections. Representatives from all supernatural factions were gathered, tension thick in the air.

Angelo squeezed Andrea's hand one last time before they entered. "Together?" he asked. Andrea nodded; her chin held high. "Together." And with that, they stepped into the room, ready to face whatever challenges the new era might bring – as partners, as leaders, and as the beating heart of a supernatural community on the brink of monumental change.

Epilogue: A New Dawn

The sultry New Orleans summer gave way to a crisp autumn as the city gradually recovered from Sapphira's reign of terror. Weeks turned into months, and the French Quarter began to pulse once more with its characteristic blend of music, magic, and mystery. Angelo and Andrea found themselves at the heart of the reconstruction efforts, both physical and supernatural.

On a mild October evening, they strolled hand in hand down Bourbon Street, pausing to appreciate the lively scene around them. Street musicians filled the air with jazz, their soulful melodies intertwining with the scent of spicy jambalaya and sweet beignets. The gas lamps cast a warm, golden glow over the cobblestone streets, lending an air of timeless romance to the scene.

"It's hard to believe how far we've come," Andrea mused, her eyes sparkling as she took in the revelers, both human and supernatural, mingling freely without fear. She was wearing a deep green dress that brought out the color of her eyes, her raven hair swept up in an elegant updo.

Angelo nodded, a small smile playing on his lips. "From a city living in shadows to this... it's quite the transformation." He squeezed her hand gently, marveling at how perfectly it fit in his. His dark suit contrasted sharply with his pale skin, giving him an air of mystery that still made Andrea's heart skip a beat, even after all they'd been through together.

They passed by Preservation Hall, where a group of elderly jazz musicians were playing a hauntingly beautiful rendition of "St. James Infirmary Blues." Angelo pulled Andrea close, swaying gently to the music. She rested her head on his chest, closing her eyes and losing herself in the moment.

"Dance with me?" Angelo murmured into her hair.

Andrea looked up at him, a mischievous glint in her eye. "Here? In the middle of the street?"

He grinned. "Why not? We've saved the city. I think we've earned the right to be a little spontaneous."

Laughing, Andrea allowed Angelo to spin her into a graceful twirl. They danced there on the sidewalk, oblivious to the amused and admiring glances of passersby. In that moment, they were just two people in love, not the powerful witch and vampire detective who had reshaped the supernatural landscape of New Orleans.

As the song ended, Angelo dipped Andrea low, their faces inches apart. The world seemed to stand still as they gazed into each other's eyes, the love between them almost palpable.

"I love you," Angelo whispered, his cool breath fanning across Andrea's flushed cheeks.

"I love you too," she replied, her voice filled with emotion.

They made their way back to Andrea's apartment, the weight of their responsibilities momentarily lifted. As Andrea unlocked the door, Angelo's hand on the small of her back sent a shiver down her spine. The tension that had been building between them all day finally reached its breaking point.

Once inside, Angelo cupped Andrea's face gently, his amber eyes meeting her green ones. "Whatever the future holds," he whispered, "know that I love you, Andrea. More than I've ever loved anyone in all my centuries."

Andrea's response was to pull him into a passionate kiss. As their lips met, the world around them seemed to fade away. Clothes were shed as they made their way to the bedroom, hands exploring familiar yet still exciting territory.

In the soft glow of candlelight, they came together, their bodies moving in perfect synchronization. It was a joining of not just flesh, but of souls - vampire and witch, united in love and purpose. Angelo marveled at the softness of Andrea's skin, the way her body fit perfectly against his. Andrea reveled in the strength of Angelo's embrace, the cool touch of his skin a delicious contrast to the heat building between them.

Their lovemaking was tender and passionate, a physical expression of the deep bond they shared. Every touch, every kiss was charged with emotion, reaffirming their connection in the most intimate way possible. As they reached the heights of pleasure together, it felt like magic itself was flowing through them, binding them even closer.

Afterwards, they lay entwined, basking in the afterglow. Angelo traced lazy patterns on Andrea's back as she rested her head on his chest, listening to the steady, slow beat of his heart.

"What are you thinking about?" Andrea asked, breaking the comfortable silence.

Angelo's hand stilled for a moment before resuming its gentle caress. "The future," he admitted. "Our future."

Andrea propped herself up on an elbow, looking into his eyes. "And what do you see?"

"I see us," Angelo began, his voice soft but filled with conviction. "Leading the supernatural community into a new era of peace and cooperation. I see us building a home together, maybe even..." he hesitated, then continued, "maybe even starting a family, if that's something you want."

Andrea's eyes widened in surprise. "A family? But how... I mean, with you being a vampire..."

Angelo chuckled. "There are ways, my love. Adoption, magical means... we have options, if that's a path you want to explore."

Andrea's face softened, a smile spreading across her lips. "I never thought... I mean, with everything that's happened, I didn't dare hope for something so normal."

"We've earned some normalcy, don't you think?" Angelo said, tucking a strand of hair behind her ear. "We've faced down ancient evils, reformed an entire supernatural society. I think we can handle a little domestic bliss."

Andrea laughed, the sound light and carefree. "Domestic bliss with a vampire detective. My mother would have a fit."

"Speaking of family," Angelo said, his tone turning serious. "I was thinking... maybe it's time I formally introduced myself to your coven. As your partner, in every sense of the word."

Andrea's breath caught in her throat. "Angelo, are you saying..."

He nodded, reaching over to the nightstand and pulling out a small velvet box. "Andrea Deveraux, will you marry me? Will you be my partner in life, in magic, in everything?"

Tears welled up in Andrea's eyes as Angelo opened the box, revealing a stunning ring. The band was white gold, intricately carved with protective runes. Set in the center was a moonstone, flanked by two small diamonds.

"It's beautiful," Andrea breathed. "Yes, Angelo. Yes, I'll marry you."

As Angelo slipped the ring onto her finger, they both felt a surge of magical energy. The moonstone glowed softly, sealing their bond in more ways than one.

They sealed their engagement with another passionate kiss, losing themselves in each other once more. As dawn approached, they lay together, discussing their plans for the future in excited whispers.

"We'll need to find a bigger place," Andrea mused. "Somewhere with room for a library, and maybe a greenhouse for my herbs."

Angelo nodded. "And a secure space for my detective work. Perhaps a property on the edge of the Quarter? Close enough to stay connected, but with some privacy?"

"Oh, and we'll need a room for magical practice," Andrea added. "Somewhere we can work on spells without worrying about blowing up the kitchen."

Angelo chuckled. "Again, you mean?"

Andrea swatted his arm playfully. "That was one time, and it was your fault for distracting me."

As they continued to plan, their conversation drifted to more serious topics.

"What about the vampire community?" Andrea asked. "How do you think they'll react to our marriage?"

Angelo sighed. "It won't be easy. There are still those who cling to the old ways, who see any alliance with witches as a betrayal. But there are others who are ready for change. We'll face opposition, but we'll also have supporters."

Andrea nodded thoughtfully. "And my coven... well, they've come around to you, but a marriage might be pushing it for some of the elders."

"We'll face it together," Angelo assured her. "Our union can be a symbol of the new era we're trying to build. A bridge between our two worlds."

They discussed potential wedding plans, debating the merits of a traditional ceremony versus something more uniquely suited to their supernatural status. They talked about honeymoon destinations, Angelo suggesting romantic European cities he'd visited in his long life, while Andrea lobbied for more exotic, magically significant locations.

As the first rays of sunlight began to peek through the curtains, Angelo, protected by his unique ability to withstand daylight, watched as the golden glow illuminated Andrea's face. She looked radiant, her hair tousled from their lovemaking, her eyes bright with happiness and hope for the future.

The morning light caught his gaze through the window, drawing it to the distant spire of St. Louis Cathedral where his immortal journey had begun centuries ago—no longer a symbol of his bondage to Sapphira, but a monument to how far he had come."

"We should probably get some sleep," Andrea said reluctantly. "We have that meeting with the Vampire Council later."

Angelo groaned playfully. "Do we have to? I'd much rather stay here with you."

Andrea laughed, swatting his chest lightly. "Come on, Detective. Duty calls."

As they prepared for the day ahead, both Angelo and Andrea felt a sense of excitement and hope that had been missing for far too long. They had faced unimaginable challenges, reformed an entire supernatural society, and come out stronger for it. Now, with the promise of a shared future ahead of them, they were ready to face whatever new adventures awaited.

The sun rose fully over New Orleans, painting the sky in hues of pink and gold. In Andrea's apartment, two figures moved about, preparing for another day of maintaining the delicate balance between the human and supernatural worlds. But now they moved with a new sense of purpose, their hearts light with love and the promise of a future together.

As they left the apartment hand in hand, Angelo paused on the threshold. "Are you ready for this?" he asked, his eyes searching Andrea's face.

She smiled up at him, her expression resolute. "With you by my side? I'm ready for anything."

They stepped out into the morning light, ready to face whatever challenges the day might bring. As they walked down the street, heads turned to watch them pass. They made quite a sight - the vampire detective and the powerful witch, moving in perfect harmony.

A street vendor selling flowers called out to them. "A rose for the beautiful lady?" he offered, holding out a perfect red bloom.

Angelo smiled, purchasing the flower and presenting it to Andrea with a flourish. She accepted it with a laugh, tucking it behind her ear.

As they continued on their way, they passed by Marie Levesque's House of Voodoo. They waved to young vampire Thomas, now peacefully running a jazz club since they'd freed him from Sapphira's control. Nearby, the werewolf twins who'd fought alongside them in the final battle nodded respectfully from their street art stall. Small but meaningful changes were visible throughout the Quarter, signs of a supernatural community slowly healing. A woman yells to them.

"I heard the news," she said with a knowing smile. "Congratulations, you two. It's about time."

Andrea blushed, while Angelo thanked the woman graciously. News traveled fast in the supernatural community, it seemed.

They arrived at the Vampire Council headquarters, a stately old mansion in the Garden District. Before they entered, Angelo turned to Andrea one last time.

"Whatever happens in there," he said softly, "remember that I love you. We're in this together."

Andrea squeezed his hand. "Together," she agreed.

With that, they pushed open the heavy oak doors, ready to face whatever came next. As they entered the dimly lit foyer, heads turned, and conversations stopped. The future of supernatural New Orleans was about to be decided, and Angelo and Andrea were at the heart of it all.

But whatever challenges lay ahead, they would face them as they had faced everything else - side by side, their love a beacon of hope in a world of shadows and magic. Their story was far from over; in many ways, it was just beginning. And as they stood there, hand in hand, they knew that together, they could overcome anything.

The city of New Orleans, with all its mystery and magic, stretched out before them - their home, their battlefield, and now, the stage for their greatest adventure yet. The dawn of a new era had arrived, and Angelo and Andrea were ready to meet it head-on, their love lighting the way forward.

The End... or perhaps, just the beginning of a new chapter. Turn the page for an introduction to the next book in the series.

———————————————————

BOOK 2:
Title: "Blood and Magic: Forbidden Desires"

Summary: In the wake of Sapphira's defeat, Angelo and Andrea's joy is short-lived. The Supernatural Council, an ancient body of vampire elders and witch matriarchs, delivers a shocking ultimatum: renounce their engagement or face exile from both communities. The reason is dire - the union of vampire and witch bloodlines risks creating a "Shadowborn," a hybrid with volatile, uncontrollable powers that could shatter the veil between the supernatural and human worlds.

www.ingramcontent.com/pod-product-compliance
Lightning Source LLC
LaVergne TN
LVHW012026060526
838201LV00061B/4481